And When I Die

Loni Friddle

iUniverse, Inc.
Bloomington

And When I Die

iUniverse books may be ordered through booksellers or by contacting:

iUniverse
1663 Liberty Drive
Bloomington, IN 47403
www.iuniverse.com
1-800-Authors (1-800-288-4677)

ISBN: 978-1-4759-0598-4 (sc)
ISBN: 978-1-4759-0597-7 (hc)
ISBN: 978-1-4759-0596-0 (e)

Library of Congress Control Number: 2012905235

Printed in the United States of America

iUniverse rev. date: 5/23/2012

For the grandchildren.
May they achieve all their goals.

Births have brought us richness and variety,
And other births will bring us richness and variety...
This day before dawn I ascended a hill and look'd at the crowded heaven,
And I said to my Spirit, When we become enfolders of those orbs, and the pleasure
and knowledge of everything in them, shall we be fill'd and satisfied then?
And my Spirit said, No, we but level that lift, to pass and continue beyond.

Walt Whitman, Leaves of Grass

Thanks to all my friends and family for putting up with me while I went into deep thoughts and moodiness while writing and sometimes ignored their thoughts and actions when I had my own stuff in my mind. Thanks to the Internet for all the information. Thanks to my friends and family for encouraging me to write and letting me be me. Thanks to Fred and Darcy and Don who said "Go for it girl!" And special thanks to Stacey and Kathi who helped me enormously.

Prologue

Pia was dead. Quite naturally it was up to her daughter, Marla, to dispose of her mother's belongings. Eric was willing to help but he knew that his sister would do a more efficient job and he trusted her judgment in dispensing of everything equitably. On a dreary Monday morning, Marla brought her grown children with her to the little A-frame. They had mixed feelings about this project. It was so sad to get rid of GrandPi's possessions but, on the other hand, it would be nice to caress anything that belonged to GrandPi and sense her in their hearts.

Marla took command over the kitchen and dispersed Summer, Jade, and Noel to whatever room they wanted. Marla was completely immersed in her project of sorting through the cupboards. She touched each plate and cup tenderly, recalling special moments with her mother. An hour had elapsed and she decided to check on the children.

Jade was in the dining room. Noel was in the living room. Both seemed to have the same sensations she was enduring - sadness and elation at touching a part of Pia's life. Then she walked into the bedroom. *Oh, my God! I should not have let Summer have the bedroom,* she thought. Summer was curled up on the bed with a sheaf of papers in her hand. She was sobbing.

Marla sat quietly on the side of the bed. She knew only too well what the papers revealed She softly took the manuscript from Summer's hand and patted her daughter's head.

"It's all right, dear. What do you think about this?"

"I don't know what to think. I plagiarized my grandfather's works."

"Darling, did you know about this manuscript beforehand – before you wrote your book?"

"No, no, no!" Summer was emphatic and sobbing even more. "I can't figure it out. My book was HIS book. How could I have done this? How could it happen? He was the one who should have won the Nobel Prize! Mom, Mom, Mom, did you know about this?"

"Yes, I did."

"Why didn't you tell me?"

"It was a secret between your grandmother and me. We felt it best not to tell you. Your grandfather died two years before you were born. His manuscript was never published. How you got the idea? - we have no idea. So you did not plagiarize."

"Do you also know about the letters that GrandPi wrote to me?"

Marla was puzzled and a little alarmed. Could GrandPi have left Summer a message that perhaps Summer was a reincarnation of her grandfather? "I know of no letter that GrandPi wrote to you. Where is it?"

Summer reached toward the bottom of the papers and sorted some of them out.

"Here, read this."

Jan. 18

Dear Grandchild,
Your grandfather died today. I don't know why he died. Well, yes, I know why he died. He died of cancer. It is a horrible disease. He was such a handsome and intelligent and wise and giving man. Why did the Gods want him so early in life?
Maybe they had another purpose for him. Who knows? But it was such a great loss. Who knows what the loss was for him. For us, it was a great loss.

Love, GrandPi

Jan. 20

The visitation was held for your grandfather today. So many people came. The publishing company people, the literary agents, his fans from all over the world, his friends- oh, so many friends. The funeral home was packed. There were flowers everywhere! I was kind of in a daze. I could remember names of strangers but not the names of people I knew really well. Everyone had so many nice things to say about Hugh. They didn't need to tell me, because I already knew, but it made me feel really warm inside. I really loved your grandfather. He was not just a great novelist; he was a man who was kind-hearted and loving and accepting of all peoples no matter what their color, race or religion. Oh, Grandchild, I must go to bed now.

Love, GrandPi

Jan.21

Dear Grandchild,
Your grandfather was put to rest today. Isn't that a funny term? " Put to rest."
He was put to rest three days ago when he died. He was actually cremated. I don't know what I will do with the ashes yet. Hah!

Maybe sprinkle them over the floors of the Library of Congress? There was a memorial service held for him and, again, so many people came. There were four people I had chosen from different aspects of Hugh's life to speak at the service. We were all in tears. He was such a good and talented and enthusiastic man!

Love, GrandPi

Jan.23

Hi Grandchild,

One of my male neighbors stopped by today. Supposedly, it was to comfort me but I get the feeling that the roles were reversed. All Greg could talk about was how much he was upset about Hugh's death. I let him ramble on and get his feelings out. He told me how much he loved Hugh. He told me how much Hugh had helped him in his own depressions. And Greg does have a lot of depressions! He told me that whenever he talked to Hugh about a depression in his life, Hugh would turn it around and make it good. He told me that Hugh's attitude was better than any anti-depressant medications he had taken. Yep! – that was Hugh! I'm worn out from talking to Greg. Talk to you later.

Love, GrandPi

Feb.4

It's me again, Grandchild,

Did I tell you what a wonderful father he was to your mother and uncle? He taught them so much! He would find a leaf on the sidewalk and they would take it home to look it up and find out what kind of tree it belonged to and what role in the ecology system that tree played. He loved to play games with your Mom and your uncle. It could be as simple as Candyland or as involved as chess. He just wanted them to use their minds. He even encouraged me. Would you believe that I was shy when I was young? Hugh encouraged me in everything I did.

I burst out of my shyness with a vengeance. I am not afraid of taking on any project and it is mostly because of your grandfather.

Goodnight, GrandPi

Feb. 6

Hi Grandchild,

A couple of days ago, I was telling you about how great a husband and father Hugh was. But it went beyond that. I hope that someday you will read all his books. His books are written to prove a point. A point to make mankind better. He felt he could turn injustices around by his books. In some instances, it happened. I knew he wished he could do more but he did what he could do. He used his craft to call attention to problems that societies confront. He couldn't solve the problems but he could make people face them.

Love, GrandPi

Feb.8

My dear grandchild.

I'm laying it on heavy to you today. You have not yet been born and, as far as I know, you have not even been conceived. But I do know that you are in the planning stages so that is why I am talking to you. Your grandfather's body is gone but not his soul. He is somewhere around still guiding us. I believe he is holding my hand as I will hold yours. That is my purpose. I will hold your hand and guide you. For you, for me and for your grandfather. I have this strange feeling that you will carry on where your grandfather left off. You may be like Harper Lee and win the Pulitzer Prize for literature. You may be like Jimmy Carter and win the Nobel Peace Prize. I know that great things are going to come out of you. You can do it, my darling baby grandchild.

Love, GrandPi

That was the last page. Marla sat and wept. She had never seen these pages before. She had seen the unfinished manuscript but these pages had been withheld from her. Her mother had revealed a great deal to her. This was even more.

Pia stared at the stage. The beautiful woman that she had been fixating on was changing. The image faded from a young blond girl to that of a middle-aged man. A man whom she was very familiar with and loved for most of her life. To Pia, it was like one of those clever drawings. When anybody first looked at it, they saw a young maiden. But if they concentrated hard enough, they saw an old woman. Or vice-versa. The drawings are ingenious and play with the brain. Perhaps, at first, they see the maiden. Then, knowing that they had been prompted to see something else, they focus. They lose sight of the silhouette of the maiden on the right side of the picture and see the silhouette of the old crone on the left side. But this was different. There was no left side and right side to this. Definitely, the young girl's face phased out and was replaced by Hugh's face. It was very surreal and yet so real. It couldn't be true. Pia leaned forward and kept her eyes riveted to the incarnation. No, it can't be. This is surely an apparition. Then, the image faded away slowly and once again Pia was focusing on Summer's face.

She became aware of Marla's frantic whispering, "Mom, are you all right? Mom, Mom, what are you staring at? Why did you grab my hand?"

Pia took another good look at the stage. Yes, it was indeed Summer sitting up there on the stage. Her beautiful Summer. Her beautiful and most talented granddaughter nominated for the Nobel prize. It was not Hugh up there. It was Summer here in Sweden. Pia slowly drew her eyes away from the stage and turned her head to look into Marla's eyes. She let up her grasp on Marla's hand and patted it instead.

"Yes, my dear. I'm alright. I guess I just got a little overwhelmed by all of this. Don't worry. I'll be fine. I wouldn't do anything to ruin this wonderful, spectacular evening."

Marla smiled and placed her other hand on top of Pia's. She leaned over to kiss her cheek. Settling back in her seat, she glanced over Pia's head to meet her husband's eyes. He, too, had seen what was going on and gave her a questioning look. She simply shrugged her shoulders.

Pia leaned back in her plush chair. She gazed around at all the important people surrounding her in the Stockholm Concert Hall. Men in tuxedos. Women in gowns. But Marla on her right side and Craig on her left were just as stunning as all these other people. Pia felt as if she were in a little cocoon and peering out at the world. She could not believe she was here. Here in Stockholm. She smiled as she smoothed down the noil silk on her leg. She had shopped forever to find the appropriate dress. A teal blue to match her eyes. Just a simple ankle length shift with a faux turtleneck. The dress was almost perfect because, although it was sleeveless, it came with a matching silk jacket. A jacket was necessary because Sweden's nights were a bit chilly – to say the least! And Pia didn't feel comfortable showing off the bit of flab on her arms that came with age. A double-strand pearl necklace with matching earrings completed her ensemble. Pia patted her hair very gently. It had been done by a local beautician. Usually, Pia combed her gray streaked tresses back into a ponytail. Occasionally, on special occasions, she braided it. But this beautician had done wondrous things. She had pulled back the fine, long hair into some kind of strange braid and piled it midway up Pia's head. Pia was very pleased with the results but she felt that any minute, the whole thing would come tumbling down.

Never in her life did she ever think she would be at this prestigious event. No, that was not true. It was another dream for another person a long time ago. She gazed at the stage again. The flowers that were banked on every possible free space of the platform were incredulous. They had been flown in from Italy. When Alfred Nobel was dying in Italy, he requested that the flowers for the awards ceremonies come from Italy. He must have been as fond of flowers as I am, thought Pia.

The royal family had already been seated while the orchestra played the Swedish national anthem. Pia found it amusing that, after they were seated, they whispered among themselves just as members of the audience were whispering among themselves. She wondered who was talking about whom. The orchestra switched to Mozart's March in D Minor when the laureates filed in and took their seats. They were arranged in the order in which they would receive their prizes. First was Physics, then Chemistry, then Physiology and Medicine, then Literature, then Economics. Summer appeared to Pia like a celestial star seated between the older men. She was a green nova in her sea green gown. The small diamond earrings that her parents had bestowed upon her after hearing about her nomination twinkled. Her soft blond hair that was piled on top of her head glittered under the shine of the lights. She was an angel, a heavenly body, a star and even a star, as in celebrity. Pia was so proud. Her heart was racing and that was when the image changed to Hugh's face. He, too, had been a star in her eyes- not only as a somewhat celebrity but also as a shining force in her life.

The audience hushed as the award ceremony was about to start. Pia couldn't help but fidget as she waited and waded through the speeches and the first three award presentations. They were interesting but..... Finally it was time for the literature award. Pia held her breath. Marla held her right hand and Craig held her left one.

"For her understanding of the world's reliance on myth, legend and religion, we grant the Nobel Prize in Literature to Summer Chura."

The whole audience stood up and applauded as Summer stepped up to receive her award from the king of Sweden. She bowed to the king and to the royal family and to the audience. Summer made the slightest eye contact with Pia and returned to her seat. Even though it was just a slight eye contact, it was *the look*. It was that same look that she had gotten from that child for as long as she could remember. It was a look that went deep into her soul.

Pia could definitely not contain her tears now. She huddled against her daughter's shoulder fumbling in her clutch bag for a Kleenex.

"Mom, you going to be all right?"

Pia straightened up and blew her nose.

"You have one hell of a daughter there. Your father would be so proud. I just wish he was here."

"He is. You know that as well as I do."

"Yes, you know that I can't talk about it now. I'm too emotional with everything that is going on – both the ceremony and my own thoughts. Let's just sit through the rest of the ceremony, go get Summer, and then celebrate."

As they channeled out of the concert hall into the cool Stockholm evening, Pia looked around at the edifice. She had been so excited when she entered the building that she did not take time to gaze and gawk and enjoy the architecture. The columns were magnificent and the frieze work was grandiose. She wished that she had a camera with her. She had not brought one because, first of all, it would not fit into her tiny evening bag. And, Marla had reminded her that there would be plenty of photographers taking Summer's picture and taping the ceremony. They would be able to get all the pictures they wanted.

"Look at that statue, Marla! Who do you suppose it is?"

"That's a statue of Orpheus."

"Aha! The Greeks believed him to be one of the chief priests and musicians. He was said to have been the inventor of the lyre. How fitting that Orpheus be in front of the concert hall. But how did you know that it was Orpheus?"

"I do my homework, Mom. Now, come on and stop staring. People will think you're a tourist."

"I am a tourist. Can we come back tomorrow and take pictures?"

"Of course we can. Be careful down these steps."

The marble steps were broad and wide but Pia still lifted her skirt a little so she would not trip and make a fool of herself. Fortunately, the skirt had a slit halfway up the back so it gave her more ease in walking. Even though she was wearing the jacket, Pia still felt the chill in the air. The thin fabric just didn't hold up to forty-five degree temperatures or the slight breeze. She patted her hair. It was still in place. Thank goodness for lots of hair spray. She shivered and Craig put his arm around her.

"Mama Pia, you want to put my jacket around your shoulders?"

"No thank you, dear. I'm just so full of emotion and tingling all over. Let's go find Summer." Pia shivered again as she let her inner thoughts take over again. If only Hugh could have been here. He would certainly love this. He would love the dignity. He would love the ambience. He would love the occasion. He would love the whole affair, even if he had or had not won. But, maybe he was here. His aura was here. She saw his face in Summer's face. Who knows what the Gods have decided? Pia giggled to herself. Only the Shadow knows.

2.

The banquet was held in the Blue Hall of the Stockholm City Hall. Pia had never seen a city hall such as this. It stood alone on an island and was huge and magnificent. The Stockholm City Hall wasn't just a building of cubicles of offices where you got your driver's license and checked out data. It was famous worldwide for its art treasures. And how many city halls could contain fifteen hundred people in one room?

Pia had been to many special banquets in her lifetime but this was certainly the grandest. White linens covered the long tables. Even though there were so many people, the plates were real china, the silver was real sterling, and the glassware was real crystal. The gorgeous displays of flowers equaled those on the stage at the concert hall. Pia couldn't stop squeezing Summer's hand. Before they found their seats, they went out to the gallery and marveled at the view. Summer pointed up at the top of the tower of the City Hall. It was topped by three crowns. She explained that it was the emblem of Sweden . The bright lights of Stockholm twinkled across the waters that separated this island of Kungsholmen from the city. Strains from the organ were drifting outside so the four of them decided that they better go back in and be seated. However, they had to go get a glimpse of the organ. They were astounded at the number of pipes on it. A guest next to them remarked that it had 10,270 pipes and was the largest in Scandinavia. Pia wondered where there might be a bigger organ than this. She'd have to look it up when she got home.

In her chair, Pia thought about what she had read about the banquet. She knew that several chefs competed for the honor of creating the meal for this elegant event. This year, it was a French chef as it had been many times in the past. She was anxious to see what would be served but she didn't have to wait long. Soon waiters appeared to commence pouring a fine white wine. Following them were waiters with the first course. The chilled roasted salmon with a sorrel sauce was done to perfection. Pia could detect a hint of mint and rosemary in the sauce. And the presentation was so beautiful. The green sorrel sauce filled the bottom of the plate with the pink salmon atop it. The garnish was a sprig of rosemary surrounded by juniper berries With all the elegance of the surroundings and the flawlessness of the salmon, Pia couldn't help giggle and remark. "This is really yummy in my tummy! And I want to know why the Blue Room is red. "

Summer, Marla, and Craig burst out laughing. With all the solemnity of the event and elegance, her remark was definitely comic relief. Summer reached out and grabbed Pia's hand.

"GrandPi, you are something else! I love you."

Pia wasn't ready for *the look* but she got it. She squeezed Summer's hand . "My darling, you just don't know how proud I am of you."

"GrandPi, I am just as proud of you. You are a great inspiration to me . You know that don't you?"

Pia felt the tears welling again in her eyes. She quickly reached into her purse for more Kleenex. The servers were now rushing around picking up the salmon plates and pouring red wine into the alternate wine glasses. Pia withdrew her hand from Summer's and composed herself. It was a good thing because she soon had the second course set before her.

It was presented as well as the first course. Pia cut into the meat and took a bite. She smiled. The others did likewise. Craig was the first to question her.

"Okay, GrandPi. What kind of meat is this?"

"Can't you tell, Craig? I serve it all the time." Pia had a facetious tone to her voice.

"Well, it tastes kind of like steak but it also tastes kind of like venison."

"You are very close. Actually it's elk meat. Done up with a nice smooth lingon berry and red wine sauce. Elk is a traditional wild game meat in Sweden."

Marla winced at the mention of elk meat but Pia noticed that she had put another bite into her mouth. Pia took another look at her plate.

"And look at the veggies. They are so beautiful! The orange of the carrots, the red of the beets, the brown of the mushrooms, the white of the potatoes. And they are all slightly caramelized to bring out their sugars."

Summer was intrigued.

"How do you know so much about food, GrandPi?"

Pia laughed.

"Haven't you noticed the bulge in my midsection?"

"Mom, you are not fat by any degree." Marla interjected "You just like to cook and you enjoy food."

"Yes, I do. But let me give you a quote from a nineteenth century chef. His name was Antonin Careme.

'Dining has much in common with painting and music. The painter, by the richness of colors, produces works that seduce the eye and the imagination; the musician, by the combination of his notes, produces harmony and the sense of hearing receives the sweetest sensations that that melody can produce. Our culinary combinations are of the same nature. The gourmet's palate and sense of smell receive sensations similar to those of the connoisseurs of painting and music.'

I'm not sure if I have that quote exactly right but it's close. And I think that Mr. Careme left out another aspect. Literature also has a great effect on our senses just as painting and music and food."

Summer leaned over and put her arms around her grandmother.

"GrandPi, you know a lot, don't you?"

Pia grinned broadly.

"That I do! But it goes along with <u>liking </u>to learn, which our beautiful child, Summer, has accomplished."

Simultaneously, Marla, Craig, and Pia turned toward Summer and clapped their hands quietly in acknowledgement of her accomplishments. Summer bent her head in humbleness but her inquiring mind went into overdrive.

"GrandPi. What you just said. I couldn't help think about the relationship of the words. The quote referred to a gourmet's palate. But an artist uses a palette. Do you suppose there is an association between the two words?"

"I don't know, my dear. Your grandfather might have been able to tell you. He was such a wordsmith."

"No, I got it. It just came to me. A gourmet's palate is the range of flavors he tastes. An artist's palette, in addition to being his board of paints, is the range of colors he uses or is identified with. Flavors, colors. Some foods are more appetizing to us because of the colors. Look at this meal set before us. You remarked on the interplay of the colors of the veggies, GrandPi. So the palette becomes the palate. I'm sure the creative chefs of the world see the plate as a canvas and use their palettes of food to tantalize the palates of their clients."

"You love words, don't you, Summer? "

"Yes, I do, GrandPi. I know my grandfather did, too. That's why I'm here tonight."

Pia gasped but tried not to show it. She looked her granddaughter in the eye and spoke as calmly as possible. " What do you mean by that? That's why you're here tonight?"

"GrandPi! For heaven's sake. I've read all his works. I am a product of his genes. I have grown up in an environment of appreciating reading and writing. You know that."

"Yes, my child, I do know that."

Pia was very aware of all etiquette procedures but, nevertheless, she put her elbow on the table and rested her chin in her hand. She closed her eyes for just a moment. *Hugh should have been here, could have been here, but he died too early. Or was he here? Or is he here? Or was he here? Is Summer here because of him?*

The second course plates were whisked away. Pia had hardly eaten any of hers. She had really been filled up by the first course and her mind was far away. She was also a slow eater. She liked to nibble fine food in between good conversations. There had been a good discourse going on between Marla, Craig, Summer, Pia and their adjoining diners. But Pia had totally enjoyed every bite she had eaten.

The lights in the Blue Hall dimmed slightly. Marla, Craig and Summer looked at each other with puzzled glances. But Pia smiled. She had done *her* homework. The servers marched out with the Nobel Parfait. What a perfect presentation to a perfect ending to a perfect meal.

Back at her hotel room, Pia knelt beside the bed. *Hugh were you there or not? Are you there in Summer?*

3.

A few extra days in Stockholm were not enough but it was better than flying immediately back to the States. After meeting for breakfast at the hotel, a unanimous decision was that they had to go to "Street." Street was a trendy marketplace in the Soderheim district. Pia and the rest of them oohed and aahed at each booth. There were so many treasures to be found, exquisite clothing and jewelry and crafts that were all unique. After touring the whole Street, Marla and Craig parted company with Pia and Summer. They wanted to return to certain booths and buy presents for family and friends.

Summer whispered to Pia, "Do you think that family includes you and me and that is why they didn't want us along?"

Pia put her arm around her granddaughter's shoulders.

"Actually, Summer, I think you are right. But I have the same idea. I would like to wander about on my own. Do you mind?"

Summer laughed.

"Perfectly all right with me, GrandPi. But I'll tell you what. Let's meet at that café at one o'clock and have a cup of coffee or something."

"Deal."

They parted company.

Pia strolled up and down the booths again. She knew of some purchases she wanted to make but was undecided about others.

She had to see them again. There were so many delightful wonders. She wanted to bring back a piece of Sweden to each member of her family. She wished she was a millionaire but she started spending as if she was one. It wasn't long before one o'clock was approaching. She found her way back to the café. Summer was waiting for her.

"Oh, Summer, I'm sorry if I'm late. I was having such a good time."

"Me too, GrandPi. Can't you tell?"

She lifted her arms to show several shopping bags.

"It looks like you've done well. But I would like to go back. I'm still making up my mind about several things. However, I'm glad you called for this respite. I'm getting a little tired and need to sit down."

They found a table and both ordered a cup of coffee. Neither could decide what to have with it but it was a good idea to have some sustenance. Pia settled on ärtsoppa, a pea soup famously typical on the Swedish scene. And she liked pea soup! Summer got a cinnamon bun.

"Summer! Eat something healthy like veggies!"

"But GrandPi, this café is known for their excellent cinnamon buns. And I need the sugar right now."

"Are you tired, my dear?"

"Not exactly tired. Exhausted maybe. Emotionally drained."

"That I can understand. I am myself."

"GrandPi, receiving the prize was super but I'm worried about something else."

"Whatever is that?"

"I've reached a pinnacle. I'm only twenty-five. What kind of goals can I have now?"

Pia looked deep into her granddaughter's eyes. *The look* was almost there but not quite. She sat back in her chair and thought about this challenging question. She folded her arms in front of herself. Pia knew that was supposed to mean that you are defending yourself from another person but Pia didn't believe it. She was simply thinking and that seemed to be the natural position to assume when thinking deeply. It took a few minutes of sitting back in her chair, with arms folded and eyes closing and then staring into Summer's face. She took a deep breath.

"Summer, there are other things in life besides winning grand prizes. My grandest prize was marrying your grandfather. I loved that man so much! If I would have had to choose between the Nobel prize and him, I would have taken him any day."

"But it's not the same. I didn't have to choose."

"Did you give up boyfriends or good friends to work on your book?"

"Yes." Now Summer assumed the defensive position with her arms folded across her chest.

"Why? You are a very attractive girl. I'm sure you had quite a few suitors."

Summer laughed.

"Oh, GrandPi! I love your language. Yes, I have had *suitors*. I went out with a few but they wanted more attention from me than I wanted to give to them. I enjoyed their company. But!"

"But, what?"

"I would be out with them, having a good time and then I would get an inspiration. I wanted to go home right away and get on the computer."

"That doesn't turn on a lot of young men."

"I know that but it drove me. For Heaven's sake. I just won the Nobel Prize. What more can I want?"

"Summer, I'm just talking from my own experience. A good man in your life is definitely nice and pleasing."

The waiter arrived with the soup and cinnamon bun. The conversation stopped momentarily. Summer took a nibble from her cinnamon bun. Pia sipped a spoonful of soup. She wasn't sure where she was going with this discourse. She wasn't sure what direction Summer should go now. Her own life had been pretty well planned out for her. She went to college. She met Hugh. She married Hugh for better or worse. She plied a job in the school system. She had children. Her life was normal- just as many other women around the world. But Summer! Summer was unmarried and hadn't mentioned any lovers (as far as she knew). She had just acquired the highest acclamation. However, Summer was only twenty-five years old. She was brilliant. She had a great personality and she was very pretty.

"Summer, you are still very young. There are things that will come along in your life. Unexpected things. You never know which road life will take you on. What are your immediate plans?"

Summer giggled. Pia thought it was so strange for Summer to giggle. She was still a little girl after all.

"What are you giggling at?"

"I just thought it was funny, GrandPi – what you said. My immediate plans are to finish this incredible cinnamon bun. Go shopping some more and then meet my parents for dinner."

"Oh, Summer, you know what I meant!"

"Yes, I do, but I couldn't help teasing you a little."

Then *the look* was definitely on her face. "When we get back to the States, I'm going to….. Oh! Look! My parents are here."

Summer stood up and started waving to them.

Marla and Craig finally noticed Summer's frantic arms in the air and came over to join them. Pia was glad to see them but was disappointed that she couldn't finish this conversation with Summer. Summer took the situation under control and peered around desperately for a couple of extra chairs. When she didn't see any, she ran up to a server and explained the situation to him. In no time, the four of them were sitting very cozily at the small table.

"Marla, look what your daughter has had for lunch. A cinnamon bun!"

"I'm afraid that, at times, she has very bad eating habits. But she is so skinny. I'm sure that a pastry for lunch is not going to hurt her figure."

Craig patted his daughter's arm.

"I think her thinking brain uses up calories. I've never heard of that before but she does have a craving for sweets and she doesn't put on any weight."

"Now, Dad, you know that I try to work out once in a while."

"When we can pull you away from the computer and your research."

"No. I go out walking and running when I need to put my thoughts in order."

"Yes, that's it exactly. You need to put your thoughts in order. Your brain is still working. Just because you walk away from a project does not mean you are forgetting it. Sometimes, when we get into a quagmire with a problem, we need to 'walk away from it.' We are not actually walking away from it. The brain waves are continuous. Perhaps we are relaxing those particular brain waves. When you go out for a run, what do you think about?'

"I think about my pulse rate. I focus on the path ahead. I admire the scenery."

"How can you focus on the path ahead if you are admiring the scenery?" Craig was a little sarcastic.

Summer laughed.

"Perhaps because I have peripheral vision."

"Do you think about your writing?"

"I don't think so. I try not to."

"Aha! You try not to! But, do you?"

"Actually, Dad, I don't think so but I think that I know what you are getting at."

"Which is?"

"I tune out the project at hand. At least, part of my brain tunes out the project at hand. However, the cortical regions of the brain are still in deep thought about my writing. It is an unconscious thought but still there."

"And you go back to your computer and start refreshed?"

"Yes."

"Do you like that feeling?"

"Of course I do!"

"Is that why you leave out other parts of your life?"

Summer looked quizzically at her father and frowned.

"What other parts of my life?"

"Summer, do you have a boyfriend?"

He smiled impishly.

"No. Should I? Do you want me to have one?"

"Not necessarily. It's just that most girls your age are looking for a husband and looking forward to raising a family."

Marla had to defend her daughter.

"Craig, Summer has plenty of time to meet someone and have babies!"

"Yes, but does she want to?"

"Dad! IF I meet someone I want to marry and IF I decide to have babies, you will be the first one to know."

She was becoming exasperated with this turn of conversation but she, deep down, knew her father was riding her.

"Thank you, my dear. I have one more question for you. We are pleasantly having lunch and a debatable conversation. In the back of your mind,or your cortical regions of the brain, are you plotting your next book?"

Summer exploded with laughter.

"Oh, Dad, you are too much and you know me too well!"

"Not as much as I would like to but it's healthier this way. Finish up your cinnamon bun to get all that sugar into your mind. What you really need is more energy for your brain."

Pia was so happy to see the camaraderie between father and daughter. It reminded her of many years back. Hugh used to tease Marla and Eric but in a very sweet way, like Craig was doing now.

Marla glanced over at Pia's plate.

"So, Mom, what are you having? It has a very funny color."

"It's called ärtsoppa. It's a pea soup and very delicious. And there's a story behind it."

Summer glanced over at her.

"GrandPi, you didn't tell me about that when you ordered it. So --- what's the story?"

"Well, actually, today should be Thursday to eat this. But, as you know, I'm a little unconventional."

"Why in the world should it be Thursday - of all days!"

"Oh, it's very simple. Traditionally, maids had a half day off on Thursdays, so they fixed soup which was easy to prepare and they could leave it for their masters when they took off. Pea soup was one of the most common soups to fix. Actually, the Swedish Army still serves their conscripts pea soup every Thursday."

"GrandPi, how do you know this?"

Summer was amazed. Then she looked at her grandmother slyly.

"Or are you making all this up?"

"Of course not, Summer. You know of my interest in food. I did my homework, too. But my homework was in the features of culinary arts in Sweden."

She winked at Marla as to say that she, too, had done homework.

Marla returned the wink.

"Okay, Mom, I'm going to have the soup, too. Mustn't break with tradition even though it's not Thursday."

Craig decided he had to have Swedish meatballs. He was , after all, in Sweden and where would the Swedish meatballs be better. He even ordered them from the menu as they were called – Kottbullar. They were all very proud of him. Summer and Pia had finished their meals but ordered more coffee so they could hang out with Marla and Craig longer. Everyone pulled out and showed off some of the prizes they had bought at the markets but it was very noticeable that not all the packages were revealed. Everyone knew why.

Marla finished the last of her soup and last bite of pancake.

"Well, what's up now?"

Pia wanted to go to a couple more shops. Summer wanted to go to a poetry reading that was being held down the street. Craig wanted to hear the musicians who were playing around the corner. Marla decided to go with Craig and they all agreed to meet in front of the café in an hour. They wanted to spend more time at Street but they also wanted to get back to the hotel and take a nap before changing clothes to make their dinner reservations. Between dashing to the booths she remembered, Pia sat on a bench and watched the people. She really liked people watching. At the Street, there were people of all nationalities.

She couldn't wait to tell Summer and Marla and Craig of the people she had seen but they had probably been observing at the poetry reading and the impromptu music show as well.

Erik's Gondolen met all their expectations. No matter where you sat in the restaurant, you had a spectacular view of the old town of Stockholm, nearby Lake Malaren, and the Baltic Sea. The name of the restaurant implied the spectacle for it was, indeed, like a suspended gondola. And the food, although pricey, was just as spectacular. They had decided to splurge, because, when would they be in Stockholm again? The menu was a very updated version of Swedish cooking combined with French influences. Pia opted for a sautéed pike with scallops that was delicately flavored with wild herbs and served with broad beans. Every morsel melted in her mouth. Everyone had something different including chicken stuffed with duck liver, reindeer meat and plank steak. Each entree was excellent and served with tantalizing individual sauces. They were all patting their bellies and sipping the remains of their wine when Summer inquired. "So what's on the agenda for the next two days?"

Marla mulled this over in her mind.

"I wouldn't mind going to FredMarie. It's on Lake Malar. They have a lot of craft booths there, too. I 'd like to see their rag rugs and rya and a whole lot of other things."

Summer clapped her hands in delight.

"Good! I'd like to go over to Lake Malar, too, but not for more crafty things. I want to see the Viking ruins."

Everyone looked puzzled. Craig mentioned that he thought that the Vikings were from Norway and Denmark.

"Oh no, Dad! There were Vikings from Sweden, too. The island of Birka in Lake Malar had a thriving Viking community and so did the island of Gotland. It's very interesting. We think of the Vikings coming from Denmark and Norway because they were the ones to come to North America. The Swedish Vikings went East. To Russia and Turkey and Greece, places like that."

"So you've been doing your homework, too."

This was becoming a catch phrase now.

"I guess you could say that, Daddy. But it was a while ago. It was before I knew I was coming to Sweden. The Vikings were very much involved in my treatise on myths and legends. Didn't you read my book?"

"Of course I did, but I don't remember much about the Vikings in it."

"That's because there really wasn't much. There was too much else to put in it. However, in doing my research, I really got fascinated with the Vikings and it's really neat that we are in Scandinavia now where the Vikings originated."

Pia was listening to this conversation intently. She raised her eyebrows with a questioning look at Marla. Marla shook her head as if to say she didn't know. Everyone, except perhaps Summer, knew that Hugh was fascinated with the Vikings. That's why he named his son Eric.

Summer was getting excited about talking about the Vikings.

"Hey, I've got to tell you something really funny. You know that Odin and Thor were the chief gods of the Vikings. However, Frey was the chief god of the Swedish Vikings. He was god of fertility and is always depicted with a huge erected penis."

Pia and Marla and Craig almost choked over their wine. They burst out laughing. Pia suggested that maybe Summer should stay in Sweden. Marla and Craig looked at her in feigned displeasure. Everyone laughed again. The bill was paid and they made it back to their rooms for a good night's sleep before heading out to Lake Lamar the next day.

4.

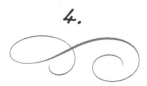

The four of them climbed into the rented Volvo early in the morning. It was decided that everyone should have equal opportunity of the time spent during the day. Marla would have a couple of hours at Fredmarie to enjoy more of the crafts of Sweden. Summer would spend some time at the ruins and runes of Birka. Craig wanted to go to the only distillery in Sweden, Mackmyra Whiskey. Pia wanted to see Gripsholm Castle. The itinerary was set. The first stop was Fredmarie. Everyone parted company again to shop on their own. Marla was particularly interested in looking at the braided and rya rugs. Summer, Pia and Craig had their own interests. It was agreed to meet at the boat dock in two hours. Surprisingly, none of them had a lot of packages in their hands but they all had coffee and a pastry to go. They boarded the boat which would take them to Birka. Pia, Marla, and Craig sat on a park bench to enjoy the scenery while Summer went off to see the runes. Then they all went to a local museum. Summer was bubbling with enthusiasm.

"I've found so many interesting things to tell you about. I just think these Vikings are so exciting!"

"Well, tell us."

"Not just now. We've got to get to the castle. The boat is headed this way!"

The castle was magnificent! It covered four centuries of furnishings and interiors. But it was a little tiresome. Not because of the tour itself but because of the winding passages that connected the rooms. However, it was definitely well worth the trip. The portraits were most dazzling. There were portraits of all the dignitaries of Sweden covering many centuries. Pia surprised them all when she pointed out the portrait of Benny Anderson.

Summer shrieked. "GrandPi, who is Benny Anderson?"

"My dear, you are so young. Benny Anderson sung with ABBA. You do know who they are don't you?"

"Yes, I do know. They sang 'Dancing Queen.'"

"And a lot of other good songs. They even had a Broadway play featuring their music."

"Mamma Mia!" Marla pitched in.

Pia looked at her profoundly.

"Are you referring to me or the Broadway play?"

It was good for a few chuckles for all of them.

They returned to Fredmarie where they piled back into the car and headed for the distillery. Even though Craig had been the one to suggest the visit to the distillery, it was Summer who enjoyed it the most. Of course, Summer was always interested in everything. The tour was a fascinating study of the way they made malt whiskey in Sweden. It was a completely Swedish endeavor. The casks were made of Swedish oak. Swedish peat and juniper branches were used for the smoking process. Swedish barley, Swedish water, Swedish yeast. Everything Swedish. They couldn't wait to taste the finished product. It was well worth the expectations. Summer rolled it around her mouth.

"Oh, wow! This is heaven!"

Craig smiled.

"I can't figure how a girl like you likes this so much."

"I'm a little different than your average daughter."

"That you are!"

Summer smiled demurely, sipped her whiskey and surprised them all with her next statement ,"No need to give too much to a man, a little can buy much thanks; with half a loaf and a tilted jug I often won me a friend."

Her grandmother and her parents were completely disquieted. Summer saw their dismay and explained. "It's a quote from the 'Eddas.' Kind of a Viking handbook. I've got more for this occasion. This one particularly fits: 'Praise no day until evening , not wife until buried, not sword until tested, no maid until bedded, no ice until crossed, no ale until drunk.'"

"And I think this to be an excellent ale!"

She raised her glass to a toast.

It was getting late and time to head home. They were all hungry for dinner but wanted to shower and change clothes before heading out to a local restaurant. Summer walked Pia to her room As Pia was inserting her key in the lock, Summer whispered in her ear. "Look carefully round doorways before you walk in; you never know when an enemy might be there."

Shocked, Pia looked straight into the eyes of her granddaughter and then saw the humor sparkling through them.

"It's more from the 'Eddas,' is it, Summer?"

Summer laughed and gave GrandPi a big hug.

"I can't fool you, Mamma Mia!"

"Get yourself off to clean up. I'll get back to you."

Pia entered her room with dignity but nonetheless peering into corners. Summer skipped down the hall to her room.

The dinner at the local restaurant was very good. They were able to taste the more common foods of Sweden. Kottsoppa – a beef and root vegetable soup. Kroppkakor – potato dumplings filled with pork. Inlagd sill – pickled herring.

And Gravad lax – cured salmon. Even though they had ordered individually, it was a communal meal.

Pia leaned back in her chair and groaned. "I've had much too much to eat. I can't eat another bite but I shall finish off my wine."

Summer leaned toward her.

"GrandPi, 'There is no better load a man can carry than much common sense; no worse a load than too much to drink.'"

Pia smiled up at her for her granddaughter was a bit taller.
"Some more from the 'Eddas?'"
"Of course!"

5.

The plane trip home took about ten hours. Pia was very tired but she was happy to be seated next to Summer. She really wanted to carry on some conversations with her between napping time. Pia was nodding off when the attendant came along to get their drink orders . Pia ordered a glass of wine and Summer ordered Scotch on the rocks. As they settled into their drinks, Pia asked Summer. "Did you buy any malt whiskey at that distillery?"

"Of course I did. It was delicious and I've packed it very securely in my luggage."

"Summer, how did you become so fascinated with the Vikings?"

"GrandPi, there is fascination in everything. I have done a lot of research as you know. Myths, legends and religion. They all combine. Studying the Greek and Roman myths was fun but, for some reason, the Vikings were more interesting. Perhaps it's because we don't know as much about them. A lot of the legends we learned in school were untrue but it is being corrected and I hope I am doing that."

"Are you religious?"

"That's hard to say, GrandPi. I don't know what I think. Studying all this stuff has really put doubts and confirmations in my mind. That's quite a contradiction isn't it? "

"Not at all. Go on. Explain your feelings to me."

"I'm like a lot of people. I want to believe in a God. It helps the soul. And then you read about the Gods of the Romans and the Greeks and the Norse, et cetera. They all believed in Gods and some grand creator. In a sense, they were all the same, but to us, they were all different. The Japanese have Shintoism. There is Buddhism and Hinduism. There is Christianity. All have a lot of the same stories, although altered, in their holy books. There must be something out there to believe since the whole world revolves around it. But our Bible has been modified through translations and people's misconceptions of what was said. That's why we have so many derivations of Christianity. Even the Muslims and the Hindus and the Buddhists have offshoots. They read different implications into what their holy scriptures say. It has fascinated me.

And I wonder why there is such a great dependency on religion. Is it a need for the human race? It's like believing in the Easter bunny and Santa Claus and the tooth fairy. It was very important to me when I was young. When I found out that they were unreal, I began to question everything else. I questioned whether there was a Jesus. Oh, I have no doubts whether a man named Jesus existed. I just questioned whether he was the son of God. Obviously, he was a great man who influenced minds with his inspirational thoughts. So was Gandhi. The Hindi do not relate Gandhi to the gods. "

Summer paused and took a generous swig of her Scotch. Pia also paused and took a deep breath and a big sip of her wine.

"What about the miracles that are attributed to Jesus?"

"You have used a good word here, GrandPi. Attributed. Attribute does not necessarily mean to believe but only to purport to believe in. The Bible is full of fables. The first miracle was the changing of water into wine. Just suppose that Jesus brought a case of wine to the wedding as a gift to the newly married couple. He didn't give it to them right away because he didn't want all the guests imbibing it. He wanted it saved for the newlyweds to enjoy later. As it happened, the wine at the party ran out. It was obviously an embarrassment for the couple and their parents, so Jesus gave them his present. It saved the day. Of course, that is just a supposition and I can think of many more scenarios for this 'miracle.'

25

"Another miracle is Jesus resurrecting Lazarus from the dead. Suppose Lazarus had a heart attack. Jesus came in and breathed into his mouth. How do we know that they didn't know CPR at that time? Or maybe Lazarus was just in a coma. People, at that time, might have mistaken a coma for death. Ha! Remember the 'House of Usher?' A woman who was in a coma was buried alive because it was thought she was dead. Anyway, Lazarus is in a coma. Jesus comes to his 'death bed.' Lazarus hears the voice of his old friend, Jesus, and he awakens from his coma. More suppositions but couldn't they be true too?"

"Summer, have you discussed this with your parents?"

"GrandPi, my book tells it all but, no, - I have not discussed this with my parents."

"Your book does not express the feelings that you have just told me. It's more of a factual thing, if you get my gist."

"You're right, as usual, GrandPi. But sometimes I feel like the American Indian. Religion was not a concept to them. Religion is not a Native word. They believe that religion connotes implications of differences between peoples and results in 'holy' wars."

Summer raised her fingers in the form of quotation marks as she said the word holy and continued on.

"Indians do not ask each other what religion they are. They believe in a spirituality. To Native Americans, spirituality is about the creator. Period."

"So why haven't you discussed this with your parents?"

"I don't want to upset their applecart. They are very good Christians and I appreciate what they believe, but I can't believe it all. It's interesting, GrandPi, and amazing. This is kind of funny. I read some quotes by, of all people, Lily Tomlin. And maybe these quotes are what instigated my book plus a kaleidoscope of other happenings in my life."

"So, what are these quotes by the wonderfully enjoyable Lily Tomlin?"

"First, 'Our ability to delude ourselves may be an important survival tool.'

Second, 'If something's true, you don't have to believe in it.'

Third, ' The best mind-altering drug is truth.'"

Pia contemplated this for a long time.

"Those are profound statements and could take a lifetime to prove or disprove. Aren't we all trying to figure out what the truth really is?"

Summer reached into her briefcase and came up with a dictionary. Pia laughed.

"Do you always carry a dictionary with you?"

"It's a most useful tool. I'm sure you know that. But I want to read you some definitions of truth."

She leafed through the pages until she came to the appropriate one. "Listen to these definitions of truth:

One: 'The state or character of being true in relation to being, knowledge, or speech.'

Two: ' Conformity to fact or reality.'

Three: 'Conformity to rule, standard, model, pattern or ideal.'

Four: 'Conformity to the requirements of one's being or nature.'

"The definitions go on but the point has already been made. Truth is *our* point of view of truth. Notice the repetition of the word conformity? In my opinion, the truth is not always the truth. It is a standard that is set by somebody. What might be a truth to me is not necessarily a truth for you. My parents believe in Jesus Christ as a son of God. That was a truth that was set by someone and people believed in that truth. Personally, I do not believe in that truth but I'll let them believe in their own truths."

Pia nodded.

"I understand your feelings and I am sure they would understand them, too. They are open-minded people. Plus you confided this to me."

"Confide in one, never two; confide in three, and the whole world knows."

"Is that part of the 'Eddas' too?'

"You guessed it, GrandPi. I can't fool you, can I?"

"Sometimes you do. What are you going to do with the prize money?"

"I would like to go back to Scandinavia and learn more about the Vikings. Probably visit Norway and Denmark and Iceland. But that is just a hobby thing now. I will have other travels that I will have to make to research my next book."

"Which is?"

Summer smiled and patted GrandPi's hand.

"That's for me to know and you to find out. Knowing you, I'll bet you will find out."

Pia put her other hand over her granddaughters, leaned her head on Summer's shoulder and murmured, "But, I've got a bit of wisdom for you."

"What's that?"

"Wealth dies, kinsmen die, a man himself must likewise die; but world-fame never dies, for him who achieves it well."

"Oh, GrandPi!" Summer wailed. "You, too, know the 'Eddas.'"

"Only a little, my dear, only a very little. Not as much as you do. But, look! Here come the attendants with our meals."

Pia sat up straight in her seat and put down her tray. Filet mignon, steamed new potatoes smothered with butter, and fresh green beans with a hint of dill. Maybe because she was hungry, Pia thought it was quite good no matter what people said about airline food. She noticed that Summer dove into her food quite quickly also. When the trays had been removed, Pia resumed her conversation with Summer.

"So, what *are* you going to do now?"

"I expect I'll be called on to lecture. I'm sure the phone will be filled with messages from writer's meetings. I'm going to keep on writing."

"Anything special that you can tell me?"

"Kind of. I've got to work it out. It's so hard that I've got to excel myself."

"You know that a Nobelist can win the prize more than once."

"It's far and few between . But I will go on writing what I feel. However, this book did drain me. It feels like I've been writing all my life."

"I think you have, my dear. I think you have. And maybe more than that."

Pia put her head back and dozed off. Summer took her hand and held it in her own. GrandPi was such a special person in her life. She felt so honored to have her in her family and to have her to confide in. Soon, Summer was asleep too, clutching Pia's hand.

They awoke when they reached the airport. It was a short two hour commuter trip to their home town. They all shared a taxi to take them to their separate domiciles. Even though she had slept a lot on the plane, Pia was ready for sleep in her own cozy bed. She dreamed of the conversation she had had with Summer. Truth. What is the truth? Is Summer a reincarnation of her grandfather? *Is that the truth? Or is it a truth that I would like to believe? Is it a standard that I have set?*

6.

Christmas arrived a few weeks later. They all gathered at Pia's house to open gifts. Eric and Gwyn with their children, Dominique and Alexander. Pia's brother, Joe and his wife, Bridget. Their daughters, Audrey and Claudine plus their spouses and children. Summer came with Marla and Craig. Noel and Jade and their spouses and babies were also there. It certainly was a houseful. Not surprisingly, everyone received gifts from Sweden. Marla really surprised everyone with her gifts. She gave Summer a beautiful braided rug for her apartment and, to Craig, some reindeer antlers to hang in his den.

"How in the world did you get these things home, Marla?"

It was a mutual question from everyone.

"I had them shipped and they barely made it in time. It was quite a chore hiding the antlers from Craig if only for a couple of days!"

Pia had bought Summer a pair of delicately embroidered booties.

"To get your little toes warm when you're at the computer – or traveling on a plane!"

Summer laughed and handed her grandmother a gift. Pia gasped as she opened it. It was a pair of booties almost identical to the ones she had given Summer.

Summer tried on hers right away. She gave Pia *the look* and said,

"'Be a friend to your friend, match gift with gift; meet smiles with smiles, and lies with dissimulation.'"

Pia threw her hands up in the air.

"Okay, that's enough of "Eddas!"

She reached over and gave Summer a big hug.

Pia had cooked a handsome ham with port glaze for dinner and everyone else contributed veggie dishes and salads and bread. Summer had insisted that she bring a dessert. After everyone was filled to the max, Summer carried her creation out to place on the Christmas feast table. It was a Bûche de Noël and done exquisitely.

Everyone exclaimed over it and the children, in particular, were anxious to dive into this divine chocolate masterpiece.

Pia gave her a big hug.

"Summer, what a perfect dessert for Christmas!"

"I don't want to crush your feelings GrandPi, but the Bûche de Noël is not actually a Christmas thing."

The adults all looked a little shocked and Eric was the first to inquire, "Then where did it come from?"

Summer smiled slyly.

"The Bûche de Noël is, of course, the Yule log. But the Yule log did not come from Christianity. Actually, it comes from Scandinavian history. The Scandinavians celebrated the winter solstice. As part of the celebration, they cut down a huge tree, usually oak, and burned a huge log in the fireplace. It was called the Yule log which had nothing to do with Christmas."

Pia took a bite of the sponge cake smothered in chocolate and considered what to say. There were so many things that Summer had researched and investigated to win her a Nobel prize. Things that could burst a person's balloon.

Yet, Summer was right. *We believe in things that are not necessarily so, especially when they were taught to us as a child.*

7.

She was called GrandPi by her grandchildren. She hoped that it wasn't because she took a grand pee. Maybe it was for grand pianissimo. No, GrandPi was seldom quiet. It was a combination of grandmother and Pia and she adored the name even though it did make her think of lavatories. But isn't lavatory quite a passé word now?

At seventy, she was still quite spry although she occasionally used a cane to help herself around. Her back did give her problems once in a while and it was her own fault because she was always trying to do more than she should.

However, she figured that life was not much worth living if she couldn't do anything she wanted. Of course, age had slowed her down and she didn't try <u>everything.</u> She was known to climb ladders to fix a gutter or knock down some cobwebs or a hornet's nest. She cooked constantly and supplied all her children and grandchildren with creations that she had found on television or in magazines. She did resort to resting on a stool when chopping veggies or washing dishes.

Her mind was totally alert. She lived by herself and managed all her own finances. But her mind was mostly alert in her use of language and wisdom. She would often put them to use in a sarcastic but jocular way. Some people might call her a smart-ass. Pia definitely would not let people get the best of her.

Her husband had died twenty-seven years ago and she suffered for many long years with his illness. It was an awful source of grief for her. Hugh would remiss and she would thank God. Then he would get worse again. He was taking one step forward and then two steps back. For the most part, she held her head high and bore the burden. Very few people knew of her moments when she went off to herself, buried her head in a pillow and sobbed uncontrollably. When Hugh closed his eyes for the last time, she was completely immersed in conflicting emotions. He had been in a lot of pain and she was relieved that he was over the pain. She did believe in a God and believed that Hugh would be with Him. On the other hand, was she relieved not to have the burden of caring for him? She loved him. Oh my God, she loved him and she was sick of seeing her extremely handsome and intelligent man hooked up to tubes and withering away. Was it a godsend for him or for her to have him taken out of her life?

She still carried the guilt of her feelings. She was intelligent and faithful enough to know that she shouldn't bear guilt. God took people when he wanted to. Why did he have to take Hugh from her? Particularly in that fashion – turning that vibrant man into a weak skeleton lying in a bed and not being able to mutter anything or to do much except squeeze her hand once in a while. She had never been able to resolve her mind about his death.

With this encumbrance in her heart, she resumed life and tried to fulfill all her life's expectations. She pursued numerous interests and openly welcomed her children and grandchildren into her arms. Life was still good. "Yes," she would think to herself and whisper to Hugh, "life is good but I do damn wish you were here to enjoy it with me."

Pia had tried dating. To be truthful, Pia did date but not in the normal sense. She preferred the company of men to the company of women. She found their conversations and lives more stimulating than most of the women she came across. Oh, she did have lunch with some special females but the brunt of her social life was spent with men. She enjoyed going out to dinner with them and discussing topics of the day. Once in a while she would have a male over for dinner. But it was not for a romantic or sex-filled evening. It was because she enjoyed cooking for other people and she liked a lively conversation to accompany her meals. She spent a lot of time with her children. She thoroughly enjoyed her children and respected them for the way they led their lives. She had her son, Eric, and her daughter, Marla. Eric and his wife had had two children. The oldest of all was Alex, a boy full of spunk as boys will be. Then Marla had had a girl, Jade. Then Eric had had a girl, Dominique. Then Marla had had a boy, Noel. Then Marla had had a girl, Summer. They were like stepping stones with a couple of years in age between them all. Hugh had been able to enjoy them all except Summer. She was born two years after he died.

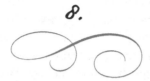

8.

Hugh Vorhees had been a novelist. A very good novelist. His novels followed the patterns of Upton Sinclair and William Faulkner. He took on issues and made them into a well-read story that pinpointed a political scandal or monopolistic environment or mistreatment of those less fortunate. His books were always on the bestselling list and sought after. They were very well thought out and Hugh was always under pressure from his agent to produce more. He could only produce one every couple of years because he did invest so much research into the result.

Hugh met Pia when they were both in college. It was a chance meeting in a tavern that Pia frequented with friends for a couple of drinks every once in a while. She had gone up to the bar to order a gin and tonic when a quite good-looking man pulled a beer off the bar and promptly sloshed it all over her.

"Oh my God. I am so sorry!"

"I'll bet you are. Just for that, you'll have to pay for my drink."

"Be glad to."

He looked her over and liked what he saw.

"Tell you what. I know I owe you that drink and maybe some dry-cleaning but would you consider going over to that table over there. The table just for two. I will buy your drink and get another drink for myself."

Pia looked him over. She liked what she saw.

"Okay. Just don't waste another beer on me when you sit down."

He adroitly carried both drinks to the table and they sat down across from each other. Pia reached out her hand.

"Hi, my name is Pia."

"I'm Hugh."

"Glad to meet you Hugh."

Pia pulled a cigarette out of her purse.

"Here. Let me light that for you."

Hugh struck the match and leaned across to light her cigarette. He was very suave about the whole motion. With a flick of his wrist, he extinquished the match and tossed it toward the ash tray.

Unforunately, it landed in Pia's drink instead of the ash tray. Pia exploded into laughter.

"Hugh, you are something else!"

It was an immediate bonding. They sat and talked non-stop for two hours with a lot of the time spent laughing. Hugh walked her home to her apartment. He stood at her front door. Perhaps, leaning against the door jamb was a better description. He did not try to kiss her but just kept gazing at her.

"Pia, would you consider spending more time with me?"

"I would love to."

"Good. I better get home now. I have some studying to do."

Hugh jumped down the steps and started to run off into the night. He stopped suddenly and called back to her just as she was inserting her door key into the lock.

"Uh, Pia?"

"Yes?"

Hugh sheepishly walked back to her.

"I don't know your last name or phone number."

"You know where I live."

"Oh, yes, that's true. So what do I do? Just hang out around here to see if you're around and see if you'd like to go out with me?"

"No. My last name is Smith and I'll write my phone number down for you."

Pia groped into her purse for a piece of paper and a pen. She handed the number to him.

"Okay, your last name is Smith and you expect me to believe this phone number is correct."

"Try it and find out. Goodnight, Hugh."

"I shall do that. Goodnight, Ms. Smith."

He walked back on down the sidewalk whistling. Pia thought that that was a good sign. *Whistling. He must be happy.*

He did call her and he called her often. They went out often. They had been going out often for two years. They were having dinner together.

"Pia, will you marry me?"

Pia gazed into Hugh's eyes.

"Hugh, are your eyes blue or green?"

"Pia, I asked you a question."

"Yes, Hugh, you did. And I asked you a question. Are your eyes green or blue? Sometimes when I look into them, they seem blue. Other times they seem green."

"Depends on what I wear. Now will you answer my question?"

"I forgot. What was it again?"

"Pia, will you marry me?"

"Yes."

The wedding was fun. Pia's last name was not Smith. It was Matelli. As with all good Italians, Pia and her relatives knew how to throw a party. It wasn't an extravagant wedding. Just plain fun. Lots of Italian food and lots of dancing and laughing and drinking good wine. Hugh's parents had died early and he had no siblings. Pia's brother, Joe, was Hugh's best man. Hugh had fit well into the family.

They had a blissful marriage. A joviality persisted between them even though the financial situations were not always that good. Hugh wanted desperately to become a novelist. He wrote short stories and long stories and submitted them and submitted them to agents, both for magazines and books. Pia taught high school English to support them and pay for the copy paper and ink and postage to keep Hugh's manuscripts flowing to literary agents. And to pay for groceries and rent and utility bills. Once in a while, Hugh suggested that he get a real job, but Pia kept declining. She had great faith in him. She knew his talents and she knew that some day, someone else would see them, too. All it would take was time. Despite it all, Pia became pregnant. Marla was born. Pia continued to teach and Hugh was a house husband and father. He started to sell some short stories. They were not exactly in his genre but they sold, brought in a little extra household money and gave him a smidgeon of encouragement. At least he had some credits behind him to get attention from the agents. He kept plugging away at the superficial stories while he worked on "the great American novel." He wanted to write and he wanted to write something great. He wanted to be a Faulkner or Hemingway or Williams. They all had different styles but he felt he could fit his own movement into the literary stream.

Pia kept encouraging him and pampering him and then gave birth to Eric.

Pia would come home from school and see Hugh pacing the room, almost pulling out his hair to come up with ideas. She would settle him down by suggesting a walk with the children. After putting the children to bed, Pia would cook a gourmet dinner and serve it with a fine wine.

It was during one of these nice little evenings that it hit him. They had just finished an excellent repast of grilled mahi mahi with a mango chutney, risotto, and a salad of mesclun and grapefruit pieces dressed with an orange vinaigrette. Both of their palates were filled to the brim. Pia suggested that they sit out on the balcony with a little glass of Galliano. They sat back on the folding chairs that were positioned close enough so that they could hold hands. Hugh swung her hand back and forth.

"Thank you, Pia for a wonderful meal. You have quite a touch for cooking. And, your know what else? You have quite a touch with plants, too. You have made this little balcony beautiful. I love you."

"I love you, too, Hugh, and thank you for the compliments."

"You deserve them."

Pia was very relaxed. She watched the fireflies darting about and remarked that she'd like to get a jar and capture some. Hugh said she could capture them but only for a minute's time. Then they must be released. She gave up on the idea since she was very relaxed. Instead, she started recounting the adventures of the day at the high school. She agonized at how there was a disparity between the "well-to-do" kids and the poor kids. (She taught at a centralized high school). She mentioned that she felt sorry for some of the poorer teens because a few of the teachers taught them with an inferiority attitude. Hugh sat up in his chair and started to draw more information from Pia on this angle.

"Hugh, maybe you should write a book about this."

"That's it, Pia! Pia, I love you!"

He kissed her on the top of her head and rushed back into the house.

Pia called to him, "What's it?"

But he was long gone.

Pia had been in the mood for a love-making but it was not on for that night or for many nights later. Hugh was constantly typing away. Tearing up pages or filing them away. Every once in a while, he would interrogate Pia again about the situation at the high school. She answered all his questions as best she could and without prejudice. Pia was no longer serving elegant dinners for the two of them. She was now cooking up grilled cheese sandwiches or tuna salad to carry in to her husband as he worked furiously at his keyboard. She didn't complain because she knew he was onto something and he was deliriously happy. More happy than her body or dinners could make him.

Six months later, the novel emerged and was sent off to the agents. Of course it was rejected by a few, but some did pick up on it. Hugh selected his agent of choice and it was not long before it was sold to a publisher. The publisher, too, was good and knew his business. He pushed it the way it should have been pushed and to the right demographics. It was a success both in acclaim and financially.

The novel was simply called "*MANUEL.*" It was the account of a young unprivileged youth who had an extraordinary flair for math. Because of his background and heritage, teachers were unwilling or too ignorant to accept this fact. They held him back in math because he seemed "slow." In reality, he was bored with his classes. They were tiresome. He yearned to move on. The more he fought it, the more he was put back into the system. Eventually, he rebelled and got into trouble. With some very helpful guidance, Manuel emerged victorious and became a very bright and respected member of society.

The novel was a great success, both financially and critically. When the first check arrived, Hugh and Pia went out to celebrate. It was a much pricier restaurant than they would have been able to afford in the leaner days. They feasted on escargot, oysters Rockefeller, Chateaubriand, and veal Oscar. Hugh even ordered a seventy dollar bottle of wine. It was a meal to remember. When the server came to take their dessert order, Hugh protested. "No, my dear lad, I am taking my fair lady to my living quarters for a wonderful treat."

The waiter winked at him and Pia looked puzzled. When they arrived home, Hugh sat Pia down at the kitchen table.

"My darling Pia, the Vorhees family has always had a tradition of having this on a special occasion. I worked furtively all day to prepare this for you. Here is the magnificent Vorhees caramel cake!"

Pia dove into it with relish. "Oh, my gosh, Hugh, this is scrumptious! Why have you not made it for me before?"

He looked at her seriously.

"I don't know. I should have. You are the most important thing in my life. You are my inspiration for writing and, more importantly, you are my inspiration for life itself. I will always be with you – no matter what happens in the years to come."

After the publication of his first novel, Hugh became more productive. Pia soon quit teaching and became a full–time mother and wife and relieved Hugh of taking care of the house and children. She filled her hours by editing Hugh's manuscripts and sought research for him as he typed, typed, typed away.

Pia and Hugh were devoted parents and spent as much time as they could with their children. They were able to afford to move out of their apartment and into a large house with a big yard. And Hugh was able to have his own study where he could work without toddlers running around him. But Pia still had to warn the children to stay out of the study while Daddy was working. They didn't always understand why their Daddy didn't go out to work every day like their friends' fathers. If Daddy wasn't off to work, then he was home with them and he could play with them. But Daddy would often emerge from his study and take Eric and Marla out back to play ball or to the store to get ice cream. It seemed like no time at all had passed when Marla was graduating from high school. And then it was Eric's turn. Both children went on to college. Hugh's novels were producing enough revenue so that they could pick any university they wanted. Luckily, both Marla and Eric stayed close to home. And then, Marla got married. Her husband's background was Polish and the wedding was an even bigger party than Pia and Hugh's wedding. A year later, Marla was pregnant. Then Eric got married. Then Eric's wife had a baby. Then Marla had another baby. Then Eric's wife had another baby. Pia and Hugh adored the grandchildren. Times were looking good. But like all good things, bad times also fall.

Pia was at his bedside when he died. They both knew that death was imminent. Hugh held her hand. He was not afraid but she was. How could she lose this word technician, this Adonis, this fidus Achates, her very soul. He saw her eyes and looked deeply into them. She felt like he was entering her entire presence. He released his hand from hers and put his fingers to her lips.

"Don't be afraid my darling. Just remember 'one child.'"

41

He died. He just closed his eyes. His hand had dropped to the side of the bed. Pia picked it up and held it next to her cheek and sobbed. She sat and thought about "one child." What was he talking about? Was he delirious?

She didn't bother to ring the bell for the nurses or doctors right away. She just wanted to be there with him. Just hold his hand and let it all out. She knew he was gone and there was nothing she could do or all the King's men could do. He was gone. He would not see Marla's children or Eric's children grow to be adults and learn love or get in trouble or, or, or....

She put his hand back on the bed and put her head down on it. Yes, she must have faith. Wherever he had gone, he would still see the children and grandchildren and guide them in his own way. Yes, she must believe.

It took about ten minutes for her to regain her composure and then, finally, she pulled the cord to bring the attendants. They came rushing in.

"He's dead."

It was stated very stoically. There was nothing more she could do. One of the nurses put her arms around Pia. She accepted the warmth and the comfort but broke away.

"I need to call my children."

The nurse led her to a station where she could call privately on her cell phone. She didn't know how they got to the hospital so quickly. She had had barely enough time to go to the ladies room and throw some water on her face. Her emotions were completely depleted. But she needed her strength to deal with her son and daughter and make arrangements.

They were all led into a private room with the coroner. Where did he come from? But he was there. Pia sat at a table with the coroner and Marla and Eric. It was surreal. Funeral arrangements were made, Marla and Eric adding their contributions with reddened eyes.

Pia felt a huge headache coming on and put her head down on the table over her folded arms. Eric volunteered to drive her home and take her back in the morning to pick up her car. She accepted.

Back at the house, Eric fixed her a glass of wine. She thanked him and turned down a suggestion of sleeping pills. She fell asleep on the sofa and didn't realize that Eric had spent the night at her home. She woke up before he did and was surprised to see her son's handsome body sprawled out on her bed. She tiptoed into the bathroom to freshen up and then went to fix a pot of coffee. Perhaps it was the aroma of the coffee or maybe she just made too much noise but Eric was soon sitting at the kitchen table with her.

"You didn't need to spend the night."

"I know that. I just felt like I should."

"Well, have some coffee. Want some breakfast?"

"Maybe just some toast. I'll make some for you and me. Okay?"

"That would be great, hon. What time are we supposed to be at the funeral home?"

"In a couple of hours. Let's relax and have our coffee now. And then you need to pick out some clothes for Dad to wear in his casket."

"Oh my God! I forgot. What do you think? A sweater and some jeans?"

"That's what people will remember Dad wearing so I think it's a good choice."

"Maybe khaki pants. That would be a little more formal."

"No, Mom, jeans are good. That's what Dad always wore."

"Are you sure?"

"I'm sure."

The next three days were a daze for Pia. Planning the funeral consumed most of the first day. The viewing was held on the second day. Then, the funeral was on the third day. She kept up as best as she could. It was good to be busy and take care of details. She had to dust and vacuum her house because people would be coming in. She had to select outfits for herself and make herself look presentable.

She controlled herself well at the viewing and the funeral. Her biggest problem was remembering names. There were their friends and relatives and neighbors and there were the literary people from

New York. It was the people that she knew best whose names she forgot.

People came over to her house afterwards. Someone had supplied enough food to feed an army and Pia had no idea where it came from. But it was there and Pia was grateful, although she didn't have much of an appetite.

Then, abruptly, everyone was gone. All the people from New York were gone. All the friends and relatives and neighbors were gone. She was all by herself. Even Eric and Marla were gone. She slightly remembered them asking something about would she be okay by herself and she said yes. But here she was by herself. Hugh was gone. She was totally by herself.

She poured a glass of wine and sat on the patio. All she could think of was the Otis Redding song, "Sitting on the Dock of the Bay." And then she thought of "one child" and wondered what Hugh had meant by that. She fell asleep in the patio chair.

A couple of years after Hugh died, Pia moved out of their comfortable house and moved into one that was even more comfortable for her. She had found a little A-frame on about two acres. There was a little farm pond and lots of trees. It was best not to be constantly surrounded by the memories of Hugh, but they still moved with her, in the matter of personal belongings and brain images. She knew she couldn't get rid of the presence of Hugh, nor did she want to. But this house was all hers – to pursue her own life now. She decorated in a way that suited just her. Not in the ways that she and Hugh had compromised on in their former home.

The house she sold was worth enough so that she could buy the little A-frame outright. No more mortgages for her. But she really didn't have to worry about finances too much. The royalties from Hugh's books set her up pretty well financially. She was not a materialistic person and didn't demand too much in her life and well-being.

She did have a large deck added to the A-frame and enjoyed her morning cup of coffee out there when weather permitted. She loved throwing bread to the ducks that frequented the pond. It became such a habit that she knew all the different ducks by sight and had named most of them.

The land was well landscaped and she enjoyed keeping it spruce and neat. She kept buying more and more potted plants to put on the deck. The tending of the land and the potted plants and maintaining her house kept her busy for a while. Plus, Marla had given birth to another child, Summer. Pia would lend a hand to Marla whenever she could. Baby-sitting or picking up things at the store for Marla. It was a chore for Marla to carry her three children out to run errands.

These were little people and mothers just couldn't rush in and out of an establishment easily with three little babies hanging on to them. Pia enjoyed cooking and would make a stew or casserole and share it with Marla or Eric. But that was still not filling up all the time she had on her hands. She began substitute teaching. It gave her a job from which she could earn a little extra pocket money and feel important to society. She enjoyed the students and they seemed to enjoy her. She was able to get out into the work force and meet more people, but she could pick and choose her jobs. Even though she still sobbed in her pillow over Hugh's death, the fact of his death was easing up on her. She accepted it as a part of life and you have to go on with life.

9.

S ummer had given her mother quite a hard time in the delivery room. She was a longgggg time in delivery. Marla had called Pia as soon as she had headed to the hospital and Pia packed up a book to spend time waiting for the new arrival. She waited and waited and waited. Unforunately, she did not get much of her book read. She paced the floor and glimpsed at the television programming provided in the visitors' waiting room. Once in a while, Marla's husband, Craig, would come out and give reports.

"It's not going anywhere right now."

Pia knew that there was nothing she could do but fret so she returned home to wait. And wait. And wait. And wait. It was many hours later when Pia got the call from Craig. He was excited, of course.

"It's another girl, GrandPi!"

"How is Marla?"

"She's fine but exhausted. They finally had to do a C-section."

"My poor baby. Is she disappointed that she couldn't deliver naturally?"

"Yes, but it was becoming too hard. She was losing blood from all the straining. It was best that they took it. Both for Marla's sake and for the baby's."

"Can I speak with her?"

"Of course, she wants to talk to you. Here, let me hand her over to you."

"Hi, Mom."

There was a definite tiredness in Marla's voice.

"Congratulations, my dear. So you have a new baby girl."

They had all known it was going to be a girl for a long time.

"Yes, Mom. Summer has come!"

Pia smiled to herself. Her daughter also had a way with words.

"My dear, you have Noel for winter, Jade which represents green and, therefore, spring. And now you have Summer. What are you going to name your next child? – October or Halloween or Pumpkin?

Marla laughed but it was a weak laugh.

"Mom, I don't believe that I will have any more children."

"Are you tired, honey?"

"Very. I'll get some sleep soon. Right now Craig's parents are here and his brother and family. When are you coming?"

Pia paused for a few minutes. Her brain was working overtime with concern about her daughter. She desperately wanted to be with her but she also knew Marla needed a very good, well-deserved rest.

"Mom, are you there?"

"Oh, I'm sorry. Marla, I'm kind of tired. I think I will wait until the morning to come. You have well- wishers there now. And you need to sleep."

"But, Mom…"

"Hear me out. I want you to rest. I will have the rest of my life to see your new baby and enjoy your new baby."

"Are you sure?"

"Yes, I'm sure. The best has been done. You are healthy and the baby is healthy. That's what I wanted to hear. Now as soon as Craig's family leave, you send him packing too and turn off your lights."

"You'll be here in the morning?"

"Of course – with bells on. Goodnight, my dear, and don't let the bed bugs bite."

"Goodnight, Mom. I love you."

"I love you , too."

Pia put the phone back on the cradle and said a small prayer of thanks to her God. Then she quietly whispered to Hugh. "Hugh, isn't it great? I am so happy that everything is okay. I was so concerned for a while because it was taking so long. But I have a feeling that this child is going to be special. Goodnight, my dear."

Pia was at the hospital first thing in the morning. Marla still looked a little tired but was happy to see her Mother. The baby, Summer, was lying in a bassinet beside Marla's bed. She was swaddled tightly in a hospital blanket and had a cap on her head. All Pia could see was the little tiny face.

"Marla, does she have all her fingers and toes?"

Pia grinned mischievously.

"Of course, Mom."

"I can't see her eyes. What color are they?"

"She hasn't opened them much but I think they are blue."

"Just like yours."

Pia gave her daughter a big hug and kiss on the cheek and settled into the easy chair next to the hospital bed.

"So, Marla, did you get much rest last night?"

"Somewhat."

"What do you mean ----somewhat?"

"Well, Summer had to be fed during the night. And the nurses kept coming in to take my vitals and so on and so on."

"What are the so ons?"

"I'm a little concerned."

Pia wrinkled her brow and looked Marla straight in the face.

"Concerned about what?"

"Well, Summer doesn't seem to want to nurse."

"You didn't have any problem with the other children that I know of."

"No, they took to it quite naturally."

"Your breasts are not dried up?"

"Nope."

"What's happening?"

"I put her to my breast and she turns away. It's odd."

"So how is she being fed?"

"I'm giving her formula."

"And she takes that?"

"Oh, quite well. She's a greedy little pig."

"Then don't worry about it."

Marla frowned.

"I know that but I want to nurse. It's better for the child. And this is weird."

"Honey, as long as she's healthy – that's all that matters."

"I know that Mom, but I don't understand."

"Don't try to. Just count your blessings."

"I know . But I'm going to keep on trying. In the meantime, my breasts are very sore."

"Didn't they give you a shot."

"I turned it down. I want to keep trying."

" Marla, I know you want to nurse but don't wait too long. You are going to be very sore"

Pia smiled at her daughter.

"I'll bet you have some very appealing cleavage right now."

Marla laughed.

"Yep, probably do but nobody can come near it. They're just too damn sore."

Pia changed the subject.

"Have you had breakfast?"

"I had a glass of juice and part of a muffin."

"You need to eat."

"It was a giant muffin."

"You still need to eat."

"Do you want to hold Summer, Mom?"

"Can I?"

"Of course you can."

"But she's so delicate."

"You can hold her, Mom."

Pia got out of the chair, walked over to the side of the bassinet and looked in.

"She's so tiny, Marla."

"She's an infant. But she's not too tiny. Her weight and height are what they should be."

"Okay. You would think that after having you and Eric and four grandchildren, I would be used to this."

"Yes, you should be. Now go sit down with her."

Pia gently lifted the child out of the bassinet and , as gracefully as she could, sat down in the big chair. The infant began to whimper.

"Oh dear, Marla. I don't think Summer likes me."

"On the contrary, Mom. I think she's saying 'Here I am, GrandPi."

10.

P ia first noticed it on Summer's second birthday.

Marla had invited all the family and had fixed pulled pork barbecue and pasta salad in addition to the standard cake and ice cream. Everyone was having a good time, especially Summer. Her cousins and siblings had helped her unwrap all her presents and she couldn't decide which toy to play with first. Pia laughed with pleasure as she observed how all the children got along so well together and doted on Summer, the youngest of them all.

It was getting well into the evening and time for all children to be getting to bed. Almost everyone had left. Pia stayed behind to help Marla clean up the mess. Pia was a little tired herself but remained just a few minutes longer to finish her glass of wine.

Marla was chasing the children around the house to get them ready for bed. Craig helped her out as he grabbed children when they ran past him. He was good with the children. He swooped up little Summer.

"Summer, did you thank GrandPi for your presents?"

Summer shook her head and Craig put her down gently. She walked over to GrandPi who was seated on the sofa. Summer softly put her tiny hands on GrandPi's knees and looked into her eyes. It was a look that Pia would never forget. Summer stared directly into her eyes and then turned her head just slightly as though to get a better look. It seemed like Summer's eyes were trying to reach Pia's soul. It was such an intense look for such a young child. Pia locked her eyes with Summer and they held that gaze for just a few seconds although it seemed like many minutes to Pia. Pia broke the lock and laughed.

"You are such a beautiful girl, Summer."

"Tenk u, GranPi."

"Thank you for what, Summer. The presents or for telling you that you are beautiful."

"Tenk u, GranPi."

Pia gave Summer's little bottom a pat.

"You better get going. I see your Mommy coming to get you."

Summer ran off to greet her Mom who was coming down the hallway. She grabbed Marla's hand and looked up at her.

"Mommy, what a mith?"

"Do you mean a miss?"

"No, Mommy, a mith."

Marla looked over her shoulder and shrugged her shoulders at Pia and Craig and stooped down to Summer's level.

"Where did you hear that word, honey?"

"I dunno."

"Well a myth is a story that people tell that's not completely true."

"A lie?"

"No, not exactly a lie. It's just a story made up that people like to believe."

"Like Hungy Catapilla?"

"Not exactly like Hungry Caterpillar. More like... uh..."

Marla glanced over at Craig and Pia for help.

They both threw up their hands in vain. Nobody could think of a myth that a two-year-old would know about. Summer was not old enough to be exposed to Greek fables or urban myths. Marla solved it.

"Okay, it's a myth that you will turn into a mossy green toad if you don't take a bath right now."

"Not take one?"

"Yes, take one. Not because you will not turn into a toad but because Mommy says so."

Marla marched her down the hall to the bathroom.

Pia turned to Craig.

"Wow, she's a precocious one, isn't she?"

"Yes, she scares me sometimes with the things she comes up with. She can hardly enunciate yet but says things too big for her – even though you can't always understand them."

"Well, I can't always understand what she is saying."

"Me either, but sometimes I feel like she is saying things that she knows and we should know."

"Like what?"

"Like just now. How'd she come up with myth?"

"Maybe she was saying miss."

"No, I saw that look of determination on her face when Marla suggested miss. She definitely meant myth."

"And she does get some determined looks on her face."

Pia's mind was still imprinted with the look that Summer had given her.

"I better get going, too. Say goodnight to all the children and Marla for me."

Pia gave Craig a peck on the cheek and left. On her fifteen minute drive home, all Pia could think of was that look that Summer had given her. Then there was that word, "myth." Where would a child come up with that? But it was the look that penetrated her thoughts more. She kind of felt a feeling of déjà vu but there was no reason for it. At home, she sat in her favorite chair with a going-to-bed glass of wine and thought again about *that look*. Children just didn't look at you like that – deep into your soul And then, the "myth." Who is this child? Pia changed into her bedclothes and fell asleep with the thoughts still on her mind.

Pia tried to spend equal time with all her grandchildren but it was Summer who attracted her the most. There seemed to be a special rapport between them. She tried not to show it but it seemed that Summer was treating her differently. Summer was selecting her as a focus. Although all the grandchildren were delighted to be with GrandPi, Summer seemed more so. And she often gave GrandPi *the look.*

11

It was Summer's tenth birthday. Marla and Craig had invited the whole family and some close friends to the party that they hosted on their large brick patio. Balloons streamed from the trees and potted plants. Three eight foot tables were set out to seat all the guests. Marla had done a magnificent job of decorating them with streamers, sprinkles, flowers and more balloons. Pia could not help but to think that those sprinkles were going to be between all the neatly laid bricks by day's end. But that was Marla and Craig's responsibility, not hers. The patio chairs, which would later be drawn up to the tables for dinner, were strewn over the grass and patio. A huge pile of gifts gathered on a small table in a corner as more and more guests arrived.

When Pia arrived, Eric and his wife, Gwyn, were just behind her. Eric was carrying a huge box.

"What in the world is in there, Eric?"

"Just a little something for Summer. It's to go with the gift that Marla and Craig are giving her."

Pia looked at him, puzzled.

"What are they giving her?"

"You don't know?"

Eric had a big grin on his face.

"No, I don't know. But judging from the look on your face, I guess it's something special."

"I'll never tell if Marla hasn't told you."

Pia turned to Gwyn.

"Gwyn, tell me. I won't tell anyone else."

Gwyn just laughed.

"GrandPi, I can't divulge secrets. Let's go see if we can help Marla."

Marla was busy putting some pimentos on top of deviled eggs. She assigned the two women the task of fixing up a platter of sliced pickles, onions, tomatoes and chopped lettuce. Craig walked into the kitchen, grabbed a huge bowl of ground beef, and proceeded to form it into patties.

Pia glanced over his shoulder.

"I guess we're having hamburgers and what all did you put into that mixture?."

"GrandPi, you guessed right but I can't give you my secret recipe for my special hamburgers."

"Well, I see some finely chopped onions and I'm guessing there is Worcestershire sauce and garlic salt."

"Ah yes, but you don't know the rest of my secret recipe."

Craig turned his head around and gave Pia a quick peck on the cheek. She patted his rear.

Marla looked up from her current job, which was now tossing some potato salad. She looked at them with a fake sign of disgust.

"Will you two quit fooling around? There's work to be done. Craig, have you lit the fire yet?"

"I'm working on it. Didn't you see me kiss Pia?"

"Ha ha!"

Marla's tone was jovial.

"I'll get Mom lit. I'm going to pour her a glass of wine and you go prepare the grill."

"Yes, ma'am. Pia, don't drink all that wine. I want some, too."

Marla shouted at him. "Craig! You know damn well you are going to drink beer. And speaking of which – did you put a cooler out for beer and wine and sodas?"

Craig performed his best sweeping bow.

"Yes, m'lady. Can't forget the important things. Now I shall take my leave and try to light some fires outside."

Marla, Gwyn and Pia laughed as he made his grand departure. Marla and Gwyn both accepted a glass of wine and then went about heaping hamburger rolls onto platters. Marla instructed them to leave everything on the breakfast bar. They were going to have a buffet-style dinner. Everyone could help themselves from the breakfast bar. Marla stirred her pot of baked beans while Gwyn filled baskets with chips and Pia set out condiments and paper plates and utensils and napkins. Craig ran in, grabbed his tray of burgers, and rushed out again with parting words.

"I think everyone is here. You girls ready?"

He didn't wait for an answer.

Pia glanced out the sliding glass doors. The yard had definitely filled up since she had arrived. The children had a slightly rowdy game of badminton going on. There were about eight children on each side of the net with a lot of squealing and shouting going on. She noticed her brother, Joe, and his wife, Bridget sitting under a tree.

"I guess we're going to eat before Summer opens her presents."

Pia peered over at her daughter who was still setting things on the counter.

"Oh yes, we thought it would be best. You know how kids get caught up in the presents and stuff and then won't eat."

"There's two sides of the story. Sometimes they won't eat because they have so much anticipation of the presents."

"You're right, Mom. But we decided on this schedule. We are even going to have ice cream and cake before the present opening time."

"Where's her cake? I'd love to see it. "

Gwyn glanced over quickly. She had been munching potato chips and Pia noticed her reaction. Marla did too but calmly mentioned that the cake was on the dining room table. Pia and Gwyn went to look at it. It was a beautiful cake decorated with pink roses and more balloons. Just right for a ten-year-old girl.

Gwyn went back into the kitchen and whispered in Marla's ear. Marla grinned.

"No clues."

Gwyn whispered in her ear again. Marla shook her head and responded,"Okay, that will be the last present that Summer opens before we give ours to her."

Pia walked to the doorway from the kitchen. She didn't mean to be eavesdropping but she knew that secrets were going on so she walked on to the sliding glass doors with wine glass in hand.

"I'm going to go chat with Joe and Bridget for a while," she called over her shoulder.

"Okay, Mom, dinner will be ready in a bit and there is more wine in the cooler out there."

When the door shut, Gwyn leaned toward Marla.

"GrandPi doesn't know about your present to Summer?"

"No. We didn't tell her. It's not because we didn't trust her to keep a secret but because she seems to have this special ESP with Summer. And we wanted to totally surprise Summer."

Gwyn nodded thoughtfully.

"Yes. You're right. Pia is a wonderful grandmother to all the children but there does seem to be an extraordinary bond with Summer."

"But it's weird. I don't think the other children notice. But every once in a while, I see Mom and Summer looking at each other in a different way."

"That's exactly what I mean."

Gwyn grabbed another chip.

"I was kind of worried about the cake. I thought you might have decorated it in a certain way."

Marla grinned slightly.

"Like I said – no clues!"

Pia pulled over a chair and joined Joe and Bridget under a spreading oak tree. They watched the children for a while and chuckled over their antics. There were definitely too many children on each side of the net and they kept colliding with one another. Occasionally, one would get hit accidentally with a racquet. Thank goodness, badminton racquets were pretty lightweight. Pia edged a little closer to Joe and Bridget.

"Do you know what Marla and Craig are giving Summer for her birthday?"

"No, do you?"

"No."

"Then why did you ask?"

"It seems to be a big secret."

Joe shrugged.

"Well, we certainly don't know."

Just then, they noticed Craig running into the house with a tray full of burgers. Even if they hadn't seen him, they would have known because of the strong scent of cooked meat in the air.

Marla stood at the door and called out, "Come and get it, folks!"

The children were the first to go running into the house but the adults were not too shy about getting in line. Almost everyone, except Noel, decided that Summer should be the first one in line. He did concede although he and Alex kept jostling for positions behind her. Soon there was a steady stream of youngsters parading out the door with their plates. Most just had a hamburger and some chips. A few brave souls tried a little potato salad or baked beans or deviled eggs. As many as could fit sat at one of the eight-foot tables. The rest had to resign themselves to the fact that they had to sit at a table with the adults. Others settled on the grass with their plates. Finally, the adults were allowed to pick up their meals. Pia continued to hang out with Joe and Bridget and they settled themselves at one end of the adult table. Joe had courteously pulled up the three lawn chairs for them.

Craig's burgers proved to be a taste treat. In fact, everything was a taste treat. Marla's potato salad and baked beans and deviled eggs were all delicious. But the burgers were finger- lickin' good. Pia was glad she had grabbed more than one napkin.

Pia was just halfway through her dinner when all the children started jumping up, throwing their plates in the garbage cans that were strategically placed on the patio. At least they were polite children, but who knew how much they had eaten. Oh well, it was a birthday party. They could be instructed to clean their plates on an ordinary evening at dinner but celebrations were different.

They ran off to continue their badminton game. Soon all the adults were dumping their plates. Pia just kept eating. She was a slow eater.

"GrandPi, GrandPi!"

It was Summer calling her and she turned her head to the direction of the voice. Pia saw Summer running toward her with a gentleman following her. Pia smiled at the man , then at Summer.

"Here's Stan, GrandPi."

"So I see. So good to see you, Stan. I didn't know you were coming."

"Marla invited me and I thought I would surprise you. Do you know that this is the first time I have ever seen Summer in person? She's quite a character and a cute little doll."

"That she is. But she shouldn't call you Stan. You should have told her Mr. Morrow was looking for me, not Stan."

"Hey, I didn't say I word to her. She saw me walking across the yard and ran up to greet me. Then she brought me over here to you. And then she runs off again to play with her friends."

Pia looked at him quizzically. As far as she knew, Summer had never met Stan before.

"Well, come and sit down with Bridget and Joe and me and we'll catch up on old times. Let me introduce you. Joe, Bridget – this is Stan Morrow, Hugh's literary agent."

Marla and Craig disappeared into the house and reappeared with their hands full. Marla was carrying the birthday cake and Craig followed with a huge bucket of ice cream. They called all the children back to the table. As soon as they saw what was going on, they relinquished the game again and came running. Everyone gathered around Summer's table and watched as she blew out the candles. She almost set her hair on fire as she leaned over the ten lit candles. Marla had grabbed her hair and pulled it back just as it was approaching the flames. There were cameras clicking everywhere.

Everyone was shouting. "What's your wish, Summer?"

But she demurred. "You can't tell your wishes or they won't come true. Let's eat this cake so I can open my presents!"

Summer sat on a big patch of grass as Noel and Jade brought her the presents one by one. Everyone oohed and aahed over each present. There were a great deal of them which included some fashionable clothes and toys for ten-year- old girls. The last present was from Uncle Eric and Aunt Gwyn. It was a very big box. Summer was a very irritating present opener. She opened them precisely She didn't tear the paper but slowly pulled it away very cautiously as if it were to be saved. She finally got to the box and opened it carefully. She pulled out a cowboy hat.

"Wow! This is the coolest! I absolutely love it! I've always wanted to be a cowgirl!"

Marla stepped forward.

"Honey, put that on your head and let me take a picture."

Summer stood up and struck a pose with the perfectly fitting hat on her head. Pia noticed that Craig had disappeared around the side of the house. Marla kept demanding more poses as she kept glancing toward where Craig had disappeared to.

"Okay, Mom, that's enough! Just let me sit here and wear my hat and look at all these presents again."

Marla wondered what was taking Craig so long. She sat down in the grass with camera ready. Just then, Craig did come around the corner of the house. He was leading a pony. Summer saw him and jumped up with her hands over her mouth. Craig walked over to her with the pony. It was completely saddled and ready to ride. Summer took her hand away from her mouth and muttered quietly,

"Oh God. Is that for me?"

Craig handed her the reins.

"Well, little Summer, I am not God but this is for you."

Summer patted the animal and kissed his neck.

"What's his name?"

"He doesn't have one. You can name him."

"I think I'll name him My Dear. Can I get on him?"

"Of course. He's yours now. But remember! There are a lot of responsibilities in taking care of a horse."

"Oh, I know that and I will take the best care of this dear."

Summer slowly mounted herself into to the saddle. She had taken some riding lessons and was familiar with the process. She grabbed the reins and led him slowly off to the far corner of their three acres of yard. She didn't gallop or canter or trot. She just walked the pony back and forth across the grass. She was completely immersed in the pony. The other children quickly tired of Summer just walking back and forth across the yard on her pony and some went back to playing badminton while others explored Summer's other presents. Summer just kept walking back and forth on her pony.

It was getting late and people were leaving. Marla was urging potato salad and baked beans on them. Craig had to call Summer back off her pony to say goodby to everyone and to thank them. Pia and Joe and Bridget stayed behind to help Craig and Marla clean up. Summer gave GrandPi a big hug, gave her that penetrating look, mounted the pony again and rode it back and forth and back and forth.

Before Joe and Bridget left, he took another look at Summer on her horse and turned to Pia.

"It's weird, Pia, but I get this funny sense of déjà vu watching Summer on that horse. I can't quite explain it. It just looks very familiar to me. Something that reminds me of something else."

12.

Summer was now fourteen and ready to enter high school. She was showing off her new school wardrobe to her GrandPi.

"Look at this skirt, GrandPi. Isn't it the coolest?"

"Yes, my dear. All your new clothes are really cool. Do you know what subjects you are going to be taking?"

"The usual. English, Algebra, Physical Science, Social Studies, and I've signed up for Latin."

"Latin, huh? What made you decide on that?"

"People say it's a dead language but I don't agree. It teaches you a lot about the English language and other romance languages."

"That it does."

"And you learn a lot about the old Roman culture. Their myths and everything."

Pia mused.

There it is again — the myths. Why is Summer so concerned with that? There was the early birthday party when Summer was still in diapers. And there were always a few children's books full of myths in Summer's bedroom.

"Yes, it is very interesting and I'm proud of you for selecting that as an elective. It's not an easy course."

"Oh, I know that GrandPi. I don't want to be the very best student. I just want to learn."

GrandPi got up from the side of the bed and hugged her granddaughter tightly.

"That is very profound for a fourteen-year-old girl."

"But I mean it. What's the sense of taking snap courses if you are bored to death with them?"

"My dear, you are going to go far."

"Oh, I've got to take PE, too."

"Of course. You'll play volleyball and softball and basketball and run laps around the gym."

"Oh no, GrandPi. I'm taking fencing."

"Fencing?"

Pia was startled. Hugh was a student of fencing long ago.

"Yeah. It looks like fun and we get to choose from a whole lot of sports nowadays. We can even take fly fishing but I opted for fencing."

Pia's eyes were becoming moist and she turned away. She started to comment on Summer's wardrobe again but found out that she was a little choked up. She fled the room.

"GrandPi, where are you going? I've got more to show you."

"Gotta use the facilities, hon. Be right back."

Pia entered the bathroom and sat down on the closed lid of the toilet. She wiped away the tears that she couldn't prevent from forming in her eyes. She grabbed a washcloth and soaked it in cold water. She didn't want Marla or Summer to notice that she had been crying. She waited as long as she could with the cold compress on her face and to allow her emotions to simmer down before she exited. Summer was running down the hall with a jacket in her hand.

"GrandPi, are you all right? I was worried about you. You were in the bathroom quite a long time."

"Yes, well, I had a burrito for lunch and it must have had an adverse effect on me."

"Oh. Well, look at this super jacket that Mom got me on sale."

"That is nice. You have stuff to go with it?"

"Of course."

Summer's eyes twinkled with laughter.

"We really got a good deal on the jacket and then spent a fortune on clothes to go with it."

It was a beautiful Fall day. The leaves were bountiful with color and dropping slowly - one by one, swirling all over the yard. It would soon be time to rake but not yet. The yard was a patchwork of gold and red and orange and brown leaves placed here and here by the hands of God in his masterful, artful way. Pia stood on her deck and waited with a cup of coffee in hand. She really loved this season but it also made her sad as she knew that winter was around the bend. The crows and the squirrels were clamorous as they flitted about the trees but that didn't compete with the cacophony coming from the front of the house.

Pia rushed through the house and opened the front door. A motley assortment of cars had pulled up to the curb as teenagers spilled out of them. Of course, Pia recognized the cars and the teenagers. There was Noel's old Volkswagen with the top down. It was painted yellow and flaunted various questionable bumper stickers as well as bright red jets of flames on the doors. Pia couldn't understand the flames or the bumper stickers, but then, she wasn't of this generation. Noel pulled out his girlfriend, Aimee, as Summer jumped out of the back seat. She literally did jump out of the back seat. No doors for her. She stood on the back seat and jumped down onto the pavement. They were all laughing and then running to the next car that had pulled up. It was Jade's Mustang. No trash car for her! It was plain white but also a convertible. She and her boyfriend, Seth, got of the car gracefully but then ran to meet up with Noel, Aimee, and Summer. They were all convulsed with merriment. Then the third car pulled up. It was Dominique's Jeep and out piled Dominique, Alex and Dominique's friend, Owen. They joined the other kids and were all laughing hysterically. Most of these youths were Pia's grandchildren but she was fortunate enough to know their friends, too. She shouted out to them.

"What in the world are you guys doing? You're going to wake up the dead!"

Dominique was the only one to answer "Oh, GrandPi, you just wouldn't believe."

"What wouldn't I believe?"

"Let's go on your deck and we'll try to explain."

Dominque broke out in giggles again.

They trooped on back through the house and settled in the folding chairs. They were still having a hard time confining their bursts of laughter. Jade was even developing hiccups. It made them laugh even harder. Summer seemed to be laughing the hardest. Pia went into the kitchen and brought out a bunch of Cokes and some chips. After the kids had helped themselves and calmed down a little bit more, Pia had to ask. "Okay, what's so funny?"

They all started laughing again, but Jade spoke up. "It's her! Oops! I hiccuped again."

Then she pointed toward Summer.

Pia was curious.

"What about her?"

"She cheats. Oops, I hicupped again!"

"Summer cheats? What does she cheat at?"

"Oh, GrandPi, we have been playing tennis. Kind of round robin and no matter who Summer played with, she cheated."

"How did she cheat?"

"She called balls out when they were in and called balls in when they were out when it was to her advantage. Sorry for the hiccups."

"Anything else?"

"But, of course. Oops, hiccup again. She kept misquoting the scores."

"Who was scorekeeper?"

Everyone burst into laughter again.

Finally Seth replied. "We let Summer keep score. We figured she was the smartest of all of us. What a mistake!"

Seth had tears in his eyes from laughing.

"Summer, is this true?"

Summer tried to look solemn, but she couldn't help but showing the slightest grin on her face.

"I don't know what these people are talking about."

"Summer, did you cheat?"

"I called them as I saw them, GrandPi."

Alex called out. "GrandPi, she's outrageous!"

"Summer, did you cheat?"

Summer grinned again and gave Pia *the look*.

"Like I said, GrandPi, I called them as I saw them."

Pia remembered a game of golf.

"Okay, Summer, I'll take your word for it. When are all your parents coming?"

"They should be here any minute now."

"Okay, Noel, help me light the grill."

The charcoal was glowing nicely when Marla, Craig, Eric and Gwyn showed up. They found their way around back where they all noticed that the teens were still suppressing snorts and snickers. Marla followed her mother into the house to help her with dinner.

"What's going on here, Mom?"

"Oh, nothing really."

"Well, the children are all tickled about something. What'd you do, Mom?"

"Believe me. It was nothing I did."

Pia couldn't help but snicker herself.

"Then who did what?"

"You don't want to know."

"Oh yes I do! Was it Noel, Jade or Summer?"

"You don't want to know."

"Yes, I do! Now tell me, Mom!"

"Okay, it was Summer."

"What'd she do?"

"She cheated when they played tennis."

Marla rolled her eyes upward.

"I should have known. She does this occasionally. Like in Scrabble or other games."

Pia put her arms around her daughter's shoulders.

"But she does it in such a playful way that nobody minds. They just laugh it off and think of what a wonderful person Summer is."

"Yeah. I know. Who else could get away with that?"

The evening was very pleasant. They feasted on the pork tenderloins that Pia had fixed. Marla had brought a Caesar salad and garlic bread. Gwyn had brought broccoli casserole. It was all very satisfying and everyone cleaned their plates. Pia had become a little worried that the food would not go far enough because the kids kept refilling their plates. Pia got up to clear the table, but Marla made her sit back down.

"Come on girls," she said. " Let's clean up for GrandPi."

They swiftly piled up plates and carried them into the kitchen. After a few minutes, all women reappeared and sat down. Pia noticed that Summer was missing.

"This was a nice party, GrandPi."

Eric looked around the yard.

"You keep the place in really good shape."

"I try my hardest. Where's Summer?"

Just then, Summer walked out of the house carrying a caramel cake decorated with candles. She set it down in front of Pia , gave her *the look* again and winked.

"Happy birthday, GrandPi!"

13.

P ia stopped by to drop off a pot of stew. There was no one about. She called out. "HELLO?"

"I'm back here, GrandPi."

Pia walked down down the hallway and into Summer's room. The young girl sat at her desk surrounded by papers and books. She was poring over an open book, twisting the ends of her hair.

"Where's your Mom, Summer?"

"I think she went to the grocery store or somewhere."

"Watcha doin'?"

"Studying."

"You have a test coming up?"

"Yeah, a really big one. The SAT's."

"You old enough for that already?"

"GrandPi, I'm sixteen."

"I forget. Time goes by much too fast."

"Tell me about it. I should have been studying for this long ago."

"Why are you so intent?"

"GrandPi, I've got to get into Columbia."

"Honey, I'm sure you can get into any school you want to, but why Columbia."

"Journalism. You know I've always been interested in journalism. Columbia has one of the best programs for journalism."

"I know but so do a lot others."

"But Columbia offers a particular course I want."

"What's that?"

"Journalism and religion."

Pia sat down on the edge of the bed.

"And why would you want that particular course?"

"I don't know. It's just something that appeals to me. "

"But why? What made you even think of that?"

"I honestly do not know, GrandPi. It just popped into my mind and I liked the idea."

"Summer, I've got to get home. Tell your Mom that I left a pot of stew on the stove."

"Bye GrandPi. Oh wait!"

Summer jumped up from her chair and grasped Pia in a big hug. She stood back and gave Pia *the look* again , even tilting her head a little just as she had when she was two.

"I love you, GrandPi."

"And I love you."

Pia had to get out. She almost fled out the front door, colliding with Noel on her rapid exit through the front door.

"Sorry, Noel."

"What's your big hurry, GrandPi?"

"I gotta get home."

"I saw your car in the drive and hoped you'd stay and watch a movie with me."

"Not this time. I left something on the stove. I forgot about it."

Pia was shaken. She had to maintain all the concentration she could muster to drive home. Once she reached her little A-frame house, she ran right into her bedroom which held a filing cabinet. The bottom drawer held a lot of Hugh's former writings that he had never published. She knew just which folder it was. She opened it with trembling fingers. The white paper had yellowed just a little bit but it was still in fine condition. It was a story that Hugh had been working on before he died. She had read it before. She knew where the context was going although the story was not finished. The book was about a family in India and how myths and legends and religion dominated their lives. It corresponded with an American family and how those same issues affected their lives. Hugh's opening was a quote from Shelley on what it is to be a child:

"It is to believe in love, to believe in belief. It is to be so little that the elves can reach to whisper in your ear; it is to turn pumpkins into coaches, and mice into horses, lowness into loftiness, and nothing into everything. For each child has its fairy godmother in its soul; it is to live in a nutshell and to count yourself the king of infinite space."

Hugh had gone on to explain that all societies had their own fairy tales, myths and legends. Some were discarded as a child grew but others replaced them. In the West, there was Robin Hood, Jonah and the whale, El Cid ; Eastern cultures also had heroes to admire. Some of them came from folklore and some came from religious stories.

Pia went to the kitchen and poured herself a glass of wine. Her fingers were trembling. She took the manuscript and wine and settled into a corner of the sofa. She lit a cigarette as she read the first pages again. She put the cigarette out. She had quit smoking long ago but there were still times when she felt she needed one. Now was a time but it didn't taste good to her. That was a good sign!

Curled up comfortably, Pia delved deeper into the papers. Hugh's direction was that some of the influences by legends and religion were deprecatory and some were nutritive. The manuscript was nowhere near complete but there were enough notes to see the enormous research that Hugh had done. Time passed quickly. There were only a few drops of wine left in the glass although she was working on a refill. Pia had read all she needed to. She gently laid the papers on the coffee table and a piece of paper floated out that she had missed. It was a handwritten note on a page of a junior legal pad.

"Dearest Pia, I will be gone from your life but I will always be with you. Look for me, my darling. I love you. Always, Hugh."

She remained there for a long time with her hands on her forehead, pondering and musing and considering.

Marla called.

"Thanks for the stew. It was good. What all did you put in it?"

"Oh. Potatoes, rutabaga, carrots, beef, celery, various herbs and spices. And, of course, the larks' tongues."

"Pardon me, what was the last ingredient?"

"Larks' tongues."

"Larks' tongues. Okay. And where did you get them?"

"I had a hard time finding them at the grocery so I shot a couple in my back yard."

"Mom, get serious. What made you say lark's tongues?"

"Because they were used in ancient cooking. I don't know what they did with the rest of the bird. Maybe used it for squab or maybe threw it away as they had already used the tongue. Can't even imagine what a lark's tongue would taste like and don't want to."

Pia's voice had become a little shakey.

Marla noticed this.

"Mom, are you okay? You don't sound good."

"Maybe it's the thought of eating lark's tongues or actually shooting them. You know I could never shoot a bird."

"I know that. And I know you were putting me on. But you still don't sound right to me. What's wrong?"

"Nothing that I can't handle at this moment. I gotta go, honey. Some things that I have to look up on my computer."

"Okay, Mom. But call me if you need me."

"Will do. I love you, Marla. Give all the kids a big hug from me."

"I love you, Mom."

Marla hung up the phone. She was puzzled. There was definitely a tone in her mother's voice that worried her. GrandPi was upset or stressed out about something.

At two o'clock in the morning, Pia was on the computer, researching. She wasn't sure what she could find out but she had to try. The next day she was on the phone. Sedgeville was a small town and the only religions there were Protestant and Catholic. There were not even any Jews. She called everyone she could think of and then went to the library. The computer had been good but it didn't tell her all that she needed to know. She needed volumes. Over the next month, she totally immersed herself in reading and on the computer. She hardly visited Marla or Eric or her grandchildren. Pia actually located an old school friend who lived in Chicago. She knew that there must be quite a few ethnic diversities there. Claudia did have a Hindu friend so Pia flew out to stay with her and meet her friend. Pia notified Marla and Eric that she was going to be gone for a week but she could not explain to them why she was going to visit this old friend whom they had never heard of before. She had some long and interesting talks with Claudia's friend. The discussions often lasted into the early hours of the morning but Pia still was not able to confirm anything or disprove anything. The Hindus had conflicting ideas on reincarnation . As with the Christian Bible, their scriptures were sometimes allegoric and people were not sure how to interpret them. Ravi also had some knowledge of Buddhism which they discussed. Again, there was a disparity between trains of thoughts and explanation of the scriptures.

Back from Chicago, Pia resumed her normal lifestyle, immersing herself into cooking and gardening and doing volunteer work. But she kept researching. It was a burden on her mind that she could not shake. She investigated Jainism, Sikhism, Taoism, Christianity, Judaism, Islam, Naturalism, Zoroastrianism and everything else she could think of. None of her researches could affirm what she was thinking. Her own belief, Christianity, refuted the idea of reincarnation the most. However, Native American spiritualists believed in it the most.

She longed to confide in someone but didn't know who to tell. Sometimes when she had a date with a man she would broach the subject but, for the most part, they shrugged it off. Was it because it was too deep a subject or they didn't want to get into a debate or they didn't really know or didn't want to think about it? She thought about talking to Joe but she didn't want her brother to think her crazy.

14.

Summer had gone off to school to Columbia. Pia saw her less frequently.

They did communicate by e-mail and snail mail and Summer always came by when she was home. In the meantime, Noel and Jade, respectively, got married. Then, respectively, they started having babies. Pia was caught up in this new idea of great-grandparenting. It was fun playing with the little children and watching their minds develop. Pia frequently dwelled upon the fact that children are so different from each other. Even though they were raised the same or had the same inherent genes, they all evolved differently. Noel's little girl, Elizabeth, was very strong-minded. Nora and Noel were very laid-back people and they were astounded by this little 'demon' who had a will of her own and tried to control the household. Pia assured them that this, too, would pass but Nora and Noel were concerned. Pia just laughed it off.

On the other hand, Jade and Paul's son, Micah, was very reserved. Jade was the most outgoing of all of Marla's children and was sometimes considered 'flakey' even though she was quite intelligent. Micah was quiet and very studious. Jade and Paul were very social, whereas Micah preferred to be by himself.

What a contradiction in all these children! Marla and Eric were different persons. Summer, Jade, and Noel were different persons. Micah and Elizabeth were different persons. Sometimes, they displayed qualities of each other but they were mostly dissimilar. It was Summer who was actually different. She was Hugh.

Pia was visiting with Eric and Gwyn. Casually, Pia brought up the subject of how all children have their own personalities. It led into a discussion of genetics and environment and peer pressure and schooling. Finally, Pia turned to Eric and asked, "How does your niece, Summer, fit into this mold?"

Eric was surprised by the question.

"Mom, you should know more than anyone else. You know more about Summer than anyone else including her parents."

"Why do you say that?"

"It's obvious, Mom. She gravitates more to you than to anyone else."

"Is it that obvious?"

Gwyn spoke up, "Mom, you are wonderful with all the children but there is something between you and Summer. It's kind of like a look between you. You seem to hold each other's eyes more. I have difficulty trying to explain it. You definitely don't exclude the others but Summer seems to have some sort of hold on you. Am I phrasing this badly, Eric?"

Eric took his wife's hand.

"No, Gwyn, you are not phrasing it badly and I agree. I might say that Mom and Summer seem to have an exclusive bonding. Do you know why that is, Mom?"

Pia had so much to say and wanted to say so much about her thoughts about reincarnation, but she held her tongue.

"Maybe it's because she reminds me of your father. She has that human spark with insight and imagination. Do you know what I mean?"

Eric nodded.

"Yes, I do know what you mean. Dad wrote his novels with insight and imagination. I have seen Summer with that same spark. Which brings me to another concept. Have you ever heard of the Fox2P gene, Mom?"

Pia frowned and thought about it.

"No. I don't think I have. What is it?"

"It's a gene that is developed in humans. Some animals have it but not like humans have it. I just recently read an article about it and it's coincidental that our conversation should take this turn. The Fox2P gene is a gene that enables humans to speak. As a result of this speaking power, we are able to evolve."

"I don't quite follow."

"Language, as we know it, allows us to communicate better. We can identify with objects better and, thus, communicate with each other better. For example, we can teach a dog to fetch but that is limited. We can say to a dog, 'go get the ball.' He will go get the ball. Now, take two balls. Put one ball behind a door and one in plain sight. Tell the dog to go get the ball behind the door. He will go get the one in plain sight. He doesn't understand the phraseology of 'behind the door.' A two year old would understand that and get the proper ball. There are exceptions to the rule but that is the basic concept. Our language is more extended and more specific. As we learn more and more concepts of visualizations, we evolve. Early man invented the wheel. The wheel turned into a process for hauling. The process for hauling turned into a system of transportation. Transportation turned into horse-drawn buggies to cars to airplanes to spaceships. It is all in the evolution of the mind of visualization. It is the Fox2P gene that allows us to speak and share ideas and improve on them because we have the ability to communicate with others and project our ideas through our languages. Am I making myself at all clear?"

"Yes, you are, dear. Early man discovered fire. Then he learned to roast meat and then we learned to become gourmands. But, have we regressed? Now we eat sushi and ceviche and steak tartar. Or we cook our meat over fires for added appeal even though we have fancy stoves." Pia couldn't help but put in a little irony.

Gwyn smiled and patted Pia's hand.

"You are so right. And I am going to have to add to your opinions on that although I know you were being a little facetious. I think we need to regress somewhat. We are battling the world for oil. Why?

The cavemen knew how to use the sun for heat. Ancients knew how to harvest the wind and water. We used to do that. Conservationists still do. But what are the majority trying to do? Trying to use up all the oil. Trying nuclear power. I'm not saying that these are not good. But the wind and the water and the sun are all there and are not going to be used up. We need to go back to these sources. There! I've made my political statement for today."

Eric leaned over and kissed his wife on her temple..

"It was a very good statement indeed, my love. I completely agree with you. Maybe we should start writing editorials on the subject. Why don't you help us, Mom?"

"It sounds like a good endeavor. It sounds like something your father would have liked to write about. Why don't we ask Summer?"

Eric and Gwyn looked at her strangely. Simultaneously, they both said, "Why Summer?"

Pia was momentarily confused and then realized what she had said. She thought for a minute to get out of her situation.

"Well, Summer is so prolific with words. She can express things so well, like her grandfather did." Pia paused for a second and then added. "Speaking of Summer and your father, I want to get back to that Fox2P thing again. If language itself is an evolvement, can the written word be more of an evolvement?"

Eric seemed taken aback by that statement. He had to think and then he responded. "I guess you are right. Animals cannot speak as we know language. They do have their own ways of communication. Dogs bark when they hear a noise. Actually, most animals have a signal when danger is near. They have their own mating calls. But, as far as we know, they don't actually converse. Drawn out conversations are unique among humans. But, writing is going beyond the limits. I don't know of any animals that can write. I'm going to have to sleep on this aspect."

15.

One summer evening, Pia went out to dinner with Marla and Craig. They ate at a nice upscale restaurant and took advantage of the patio dining. The meal was excellent and so was the companionship. She was so fortunate to have a daughter who included her as a friend and not only as a mother. Craig was also a good friend. Pia and Craig had a somewhat sarcastic repartee between them during dinner. He liked to tease her but she could tease back just as well. Marla would act like she was not amused at their comments to each other but she knew deep down that they really had a genuine feeling for each other She was so happy for that. It was not every mother who got along so well with their son-in-law.

They were polishing off their meal with some hearty coffee when Pia asked, "Where is Summer tonight? Why didn't she join us?"

Marla and Craig both sighed almost simultaneously but it was Craig who spoke first. "We hardly see her any more, GrandPi. She is either on the computer or at the library. She's working on her final dissertation for school."

Marla had to put in a few extra words. "I think she is working too hard on it. She will definitely graduate with honors and she already has a job promised to her. We, too, miss seeing her."

"Yes, it's like she's over-extending herself." Craig said. " She has always been a good student but, now, it's like she's driven."

Pia put down her cup of coffee. "I didn't know she had a job offer. Who's it with?"

"*The New Yorker.*"

"Oh, my God," squealed Pia. "That's one hell of a magazine to start off with. What is going to be her position?"

"Feature writer."

Pia was all smiles.

"That's so exciting. I'm kind of disappointed that she has not told me but I am so excited for her!"

Marla sighed again.

"Yes, I am surprised that she has not told you - of all people, but she is so very preoccupied with this thesis."

"What's it about?'

"She doesn't talk about it much. All I know is that it is about myths and legends."

Pia put her coffee cup down as carefully as possible, trying not to show that her hands were shaking. She tried to control her voice.

"Oh, really. It must be interesting. What does she have to say about them?'

Marla sensed that her Mother's attitude had changed a little but didn't respond to it.

"As I said, she really doesn't talk much about it. She just keeps plugging away. She just has this fierce determination."

Pia grabbed her purse. "I'm getting a little tired. I think I'd like to leave now and go home."

Craig summoned the waiter and while they waited for the check, there was hardly any conversation. It was the same on the way home. After Marla and Craig had dropped Pia off at her home, Marla turned to her husband.

"Did you think that GrandPi was acting strangely at the end of dinner?"

"Yes, I definitely did. We were having such a good time until we brought up Summer. What do you think of it?"

"I dunno. I just dunno. Sometimes, she acts really spooky lately."

Pia changed into her pajamas and climbed into bed. The covers felt so good and she felt so tired. On the other hand, she wasn't tired. She had so much to think about. She lay in the darkness with her mind on overactive until she finally fell asleep.

16.

The phone rang only a couple of times before, to Pia's relief, Summer answered.

"Hi Summer. I don't know if you want to do this, but I'd like to read your manuscript."

"GrandPi, I've been thinking about this a long time. I've wanted to show it to someone. Most of all, to show it to you. But I didn't know what people would think of it. It's a little different and it might be very objectionable to some people."

"So?"

"Yes, GrandPi. I want you to read it."

"I'll be right over."

Pia read the manuscript. It was just what she had thought it would be. She cried constantly as she read. Summer's dissertation for graduation had turned into a full-length novel. It was a novel, in the sense that it was fictional, but it contained a lot of truths.

Summer submitted it to literary agents and it was picked up immediately. The literati loved it and soon Summer was chosen as a nominee for a Nobel Prize in literature.

Marla held a grand party in honor of Summer's nomination. It was a full dress affair with champagne and plenty of fancy hors d'oeurvres. Pia begged Marla to let her help and the offer was gratefully accepted. The party was in full swing and Pia was in the kitchen adding small garnishes to another platter of goodies.

"Aha, and who is this beautiful behind- the- scenes woman in an apron and flour smudges on her face?"

Pia glanced up and yelled in excitement. "Stan Morrow! Oh my goodness! Come give me a hug. What are you doing here? It's been ages!"

Stan hugged her so hard that he swung her off her feet.

"What am I doing here? I'm supposed to be here. I deserve coming to this shindig. After all, I am Summer's agent."

"You're what?!!!"

"I'm Summer's literary agent. Hasn't this protégé of yours done well!"

"She...- she never told me who her agent was and I never thought to ask. Wasn't that stupid of me? I should have recommended her to you at the start."

"What makes it better is that she came to me on her own. Actually, she did not know who I was other than another agent interested in her work."

"Well, obviously, she knows now."

"Pia, I have news for you. I never told her that I was Hugh's agent, and as far as I know, she still doesn't know. "

Pia sat down on a stool at the breakfast bar and invited Stan to do the same. She ran her fingers through her hair and looked Stan directly in the eye. "You're telling me that Summer does not know that you were her grandfather's agent."

"Yes, that is correct. When she sent in her manuscript, I read it and knew who it was from. However, that didn't influence me in the least. The manuscript was good. Very, very, very good. I knew our house had to have it."

"How did she come in touch with you?"

"Just like all the other writers. She sent manuscripts to bunches of agents."

"And you're the one who got the contract with her."

"I consider myself lucky. After all, like I said, the book was excellent. It was newsworthy. It was a best seller in a certain market and you know our firm knows demographics well. I'm sure that there were other agents out there wanting it, too. For some strange reason, Summer chose me although I never, ever told her that I was Hugh's agent. I wanted to deal with her as a different individual and not let her feel like she was being pampered to because of her relationship to her grandfather."

"There's one thing that puzzles me, Stan."

"Yes?"

Morrow looked at her with raised eyebrows.

Pia put her fingertips on her temples and massaged them.

"Do you remember Summer's birthday party when she got the pony?'

"Yes."

"She knew who you were then. She called you Stan and I remonstrated you for letting her call you Stan instead of Mr. Morrow."

"That's odd, Pia, because I do remember that. I have no earthly idea of what happened that day. My best explanation is that someone else had seen me and prompted Summer to go tell her grandmother that Stan had arrived."

Pia considered this. It could be a likely explanation. But, why, oh why, did she pick Stan as her agent now? It was odd and very coincidental .

Stan reached over and wiped the flour from her face.

"Come on, Pia. Take off the apron. Let's go grab ourselves a glass of champagne and join the rest of the guests."

P ia reached for the phone and dialed. She was happy not to get an answering machine.

"Marla, it's me – Mom."

"Guess what, Mom. I recognize your voice after all these years."

"Thanks. Marla, you wanna do lunch tomorrow?"

"Sure. What's the occasion?"

"No occasion. I just want to talk to you about something."

"Mom, you sound like you're disturbed about something. Is anything wrong?"

"Nothing's wrong. There's just something I want to talk to you about."

"Can't you tell me over the phone?"

"It's really a matter to be discussed face to face."

"Mom, you are worrying me."

"Sorry, honey."

Pia laughed.

"I didn't mean to sound so grim. Don't you worry your beautiful blonde head about it."

"Gee, thanks. I'm really going to get a good night's sleep tonight, wondering what my Mother wants to talk to me about."

Pia laughed again.

"You must be entering middle age, my dear. You not only have to worry about your children but your Mother, too. You're caught in the middle."

"I worried about you long before I had children."

"Is that a compliment or an insult?"

"Take it any way you want. Where do you want to go tomorrow – and what time?"

"The Aquarium place. About noon?"

"Sure. Meet you there."

Pia never could remember the name of the restaurant but it had a lot of aquariums in it so she always referred to it that way. It was a good place to go tomorrow. She could concentrate on the fish while she was trying to gather her thoughts and put her thoughts together to express them to Marla. She sat down at her desk and started jotting down notes. She wanted to remember everything. Her sleep was restless that night and full of strange jumbled dreams. She dreamed of being lost in a forest and her panic awoke her. Then she would go back to sleep and experience another disturbing dream which was unrelated to the past one but would frighten her and awaken her. The pattern was recurrent all through the night. At six in the morning, she had had enough and decided to get out of bed. She was exhausted but could no longer desire to sleep. After a long exhilarating shower, she fixed some toast and coffee. Sitting at the kitchen table, she recalled the dreams. What did they signify? Maybe she shouldn't have this discussion with Marla today. But she had to tell someone – and Marla was the best one to tell.

Pia was seated at a table and fingering her wine glass when Marla arrived.

"Hi, Mom, sorry I'm late."

"I don't think you're late. Anyway, I've been enjoying the fish." Actually, Pia had been concentrating on the fish, trying to set her focus and figure out how to broach this subject with Marla.

The waiter approached.

"Hi, I'm Eddie and I'll be your server this afternoon."

He looked at Marla.

"I've already met your charming lunch companion. What can I get you to drink?"

Marla ordered a Long Island Tea.

Eddie inquired whether Pia was ready for another glass of wine but she shook her head. Pia was surprised that Marla had ordered a Long Island Tea. Marla usually didn't go in for stiff drinks and she remarked to Marla about it.

"Mom, I have a feeling that I'm going to need a stiff drink."

"Why's that?"

"I know you. You are being intriguing about something."

"Intriguing?"

"Yes, you call me up to invite me to lunch and say you want to talk about something. I could feel the hesitation in your voice like you didn't know if it was the right thing to do. So what is it?"

"I'll tell you in due time."

Actually Pia was hedging. She wasn't sure how to approach the subject. She stared at the fish for a few more minutes.

"Mom, come out with it!"

"Let's look at the menu first and wait until you get your drink."

Marla was becoming exasperated but she opened the menu. Pia was still staring at the fish which provoked Marla even more.

"Aren't you going to look at the menu?"

"Oh, I've already decided. I'm having the sea bass."

"When did you decide that?"

"A while ago."

"How long have you been here?"

"I dunno. Maybe an hour."

"How many glasses of wine have you had?"

Pia took her eyes off the aquariums and leveled them on her daughter's with defiance.

"This is the only glass of wine that I have had. And as you can see, it is still half full."

Recognizing the bit of enmity in the inflection of her voice, Pia took a different turn. She laughed.

"Or maybe the glass is half empty. But you know I've always been an optimist."

"Yes, you are, Mom. But today you are strange."

"Stranger than usual?"

"Wellll, yes."

Eddie returned with Marla's drink and took their lunch orders. Pia indicated that she would like another glass of wine . She knew she would need a standby. When the waiter departed out of their sight, Marla took a big sip of her tea and turned to her mother.

"Will you please stop staring at the fish and talk to me. What is this about?!"

Marla was almost becoming indignant. She was trying to keep her voice to a loud whisper so that she would not attract the attention of other diners.

Pia slowly rotated in her position so that she faced Marla head on. She took a slow sip of her wine and stared at Marla over the rim of her glass.

"Marla, this is about Summer."

"Mom! What about Summer? Is she in some kind of trouble that I don't know about?"

A wry smile erupted from Pia's mouth, although her eyes were still serious.

"I'm sorry, my dear, I didn't mean to panic you. Perhaps, I should start off on another vein of thought. Do you believe in reincarnation?"

Okay, Marla had had it. Either her mother had had too much to drink or she was going off the deep end. She took another big swig of her tea and suddenly realized that maybe she better not drink very much. Her mother was going off on two different tangents. First Summer and, then, reincarnation. She better take this slowly.

"I don't know if I believe in reincarnation or not. There have been studies and studies, both positive and negative. What's this got to do with Summer?"

"I know I'm puzzling you. Let me go through this point by point."

"Point by point?"

"Yes. Please be patient with me. I have been trying to put this together in my head."

Pia smiled.

"That's why I keep staring at the fish. They are helping to keep my thoughts concentrated."

"Yes, fish can do that, but what are you concentrating on?"

"Okay."

Pia took a big gulp of wine and a deep breath.

"Do you remember Summer's second birthday?'

"I guess so."

"No, think about it. Did she say anything unusual?"

"I don't remember."

"She asked you what a myth was."

"Oh, yeah, I do remember that. It is kinda funny to think about that now that Summer has written a book about myths. But, so what?"

"Just keep that in mind while I go on."

"Okay."

Marla still had a quizzical look on her face.

"On her tenth birthday, you gave Summer a pony."

"Yes, we did. Soooo?"

"Summer would just go off riding on that pony. Not galloping around but just slowly riding it around. She just wandered all over your grounds with it."

"That she did. Just like she was in a world of her own."

"Exactly. She loved just strolling around on that pony's back and lost all track of time. Just 'round and 'round on your grounds. "

"Well, we were lucky to have enough space for her to ride that pony."

"Yes, you were, but let me get back to another point. What subjects did Summer take in high school?"

"The usual for a college-bound student."

"But even more. She took four years of Latin."

Marla grinned at the thought of her pride in her daughter's grades.

"That was her choice and she did well at it."

"Why did she take Latin?"

"Because she thought it would further her knowledge of English."

"My point exactly."

Eddie appeared at their table with their lunches. They had not even seen him approaching since they were concentrating on each other. Marla trying to figure out what her mother was saying and Pia trying to put things in order.

"Anything else I can get you ladies?"

"No, thank you Eddie. All we need is some time together."

Pia smiled sweetly at him.

Pia dove into her sea bass. It was grilled perfectly and carried a sauce of butter and capers.

"Mom, don't you think it a little weird that you have been staring at those fish and now you are eating one?"

"Maybe I was drooling over them."

"I don't think so."

Marla cut a piece of her chicken Diablo and chewed carefully. She put down her fork and took another drink of tea.

"So, Mom, get on with your thoughts."

"What did Summer study in college?"

"Journalism."

"Why?"

"She wanted to pursue a writing career."

"Don't you think THAT is weird?"

"Why? Because Dad was a writer?"

"Why didn't she concentrate on creative writing?"

"That was her choice. I think she thought she could find a job as a journalist and have a job while she pursued creative writing."

"Makes sense."

Pia reminisced. *"Pia, you shouldn't have to be working while I spend a fortune in postage sending manuscripts to agents all over the world."*

"Mom, did I lose you. Where are you?"

Pia had a vague smile on her face.

"Sorry, honey. I was just thinking about something."

"Dad?"

"Yes."

"Of course Summer's career choice makes you think of Dad."

"It's not only that."

Every time that Pia brought up a point to Marla she checked it off on her list. Not crossed it off, but checked it off. She was going to have to go back through it and review it. Marla kept glancing at Pia's hand as she checked things off. It was impossible to read for many reasons. It was upside down from Marla's point of view. Pia had terrible penmanship. And she also seemed to have written her notes in symbols or some kind of shorthand.

"Marla, do you remember Summer's twenty-first birthday?"

"Yes. The whole family went to Outback for dinner."

"What did Summer order?"

"I don't really remember but I am assuming it was a steak."

Pia reached over and put her hand on her daughter's.

"Yes, I'm sure it was a steak because that's why we go to the Outback. But what did she order to drink?"

Marla burst out laughing.

"Oh, I do remember that! It was funny. We had gone around the table placing our drink orders. I probably had a pina colada or something like that. You had a glass of wine. Noel had an Australian beer and Jade had some fancy drink. And then the waiter turned to Summer. After all, it was her twenty-first birthday and we were eager to see what she would order. We all dropped our jaws when she ordered a Scotch and water. We did know that she had been drinking alcoholic beverages before she was twenty-one but SCOTCH AND WATER?"

Pia nodded with a bit of sadness in her eyes.

"Yes, that was odd wasn't it?"

"I do remember Jade and Noel being surprised. After they got over the original shock, they started teasing Summer about it. Saying that since she was twenty-one now, she was turning into a serious drinker. No more beer or drinks with umbrellas for her. I was a little surprised too, Mom, and I think I know what you are thinking. Dad's favorite drink was Scotch and water."

Pia took another nibble of her fish and chewed thoughtfully before replying. "Yes, I know you know that but did Summer know?"

"Gees, I don't know! I don't think so because I had remarked to her that Scotch and water was her grandfather's favorite drink. She had made some comment like 'Oh, really.'"

"But she still drinks Scotch."

"So what? Apparently she likes it."

"And her cheating."

Marla was indignant. "Summer doesn't cheat!"

"Oh, I don't mean at school. I mean when she plays games."

Marla's mood changed rapidly and she almost choked on her tea as she hooted. "Oh, I know what you are saying. Like when they all play tennis or Monopoly or even Crazy Eights. She is so funny. Like she thinks that nobody thinks she is cheating. But she is cheating and everyone knows she is cheating, even herself."

"Precisely!"

"But she's not actually cheating. She's having fun with everyone. She's out to tease them and have a good time."

Pia sighed.

"I know you are protecting your daughter but you don't have to. I am not accusing her. It's in her personality. Like you said. She's out to tease everyone. And that she does. Everyone knows she is cheating and it does all come down to the winner fair and square, but Summer has taken the seriousness out of the game and put in a little levity."

Marla opened her mouth to reply but Eddie was back at their table.

"How are you ladies doing?"

"Just fine, Eddie. Will you please bring the check? And as soon as possible." Pia's tone was curt. Marla was surprised. Her mother was usually very playful toward servers. It was apparent that Eddie's appearance annoyed her.

"Mom, what's wrong?"

Pia couldn't go on with it. She put her elbows on the table and buried her forehead in her hands.

"I'm sorry, Marla. I just got the worst headache. I want to go home and go to bed."

"You want to have some coffee? Maybe I have some ibuprofen in my purse." Marla starting digging into her handbag.

"No, dear, I just need to go home."

"Go on ahead. I'll take care of lunch."

"No you won't. I asked you to lunch and I intend to pay for it."

"But, Mom, you're not feeling well. I can pay for this one and you pay for the next. See? It will make it an obligation."

Marla eyed her mother compassionately.

"No. I want to pay, Marla."

Pia was almost belligerent.

"Where is that waiter?"

Marla was becoming more and more concerned. This certainly was not Pia's style. All of a sudden, she had become so tense. What was going on? She watched as Pia drained her glass of wine and then looked around for Eddie. He returned with the bill and Pia slapped her credit card on top of the leather bill holder and thrust it toward him.

"Mom, you want me to drive you home?"

"I'm perfectly okay. I can drive myself home. I just have a headache. That's all."

Pia rubbed her temples as though to demonstrate. When Eddie returned with the tab, Pia quickly added in a tip, signed her name and turned toward Marla.

"Let's go."

They slid out of the booth and walked quietly to the entrance into the glare of the afternoon sun. Marla pulled out her sunglasses and watched her mother hurry over to her parked car. Pia had not even said good-bye or given her a little peck. She had just rushed to her car. Marla watched as the Toyota Celica pulled away from the curb. Yes, it was headed in the direction of Pia's home. Marla crossed the street and got into her own car.

Then it hit her. What her Mother was trying to say. *Oh my God. It can't be true! Mom's flipped her lid. There has to be a logical explanation for everything. I've got to get back to her. She's got to explain her reasoning.* Marla pulled out her cell phone and dialed her Mom's number. No answer. She kept trying.

Instead of going straight home, Marla drove by Pia's house. Her car was not in the driveway. It should have been there. Pia had driven off from the restaurant several minutes before Marla had. Where in the world was she? Marla was getting frantic. She kept redialing the cell phone number and getting no response.

Pia heard her cell ringing and chose not to answer it. After getting out of sight of Marla, she had circled around and gone back to the restaurant. She sat at the bar and had another glass of wine. What in the world had prompted her to express all this to Marla? She had no right to burden her daughter with this. She was not even sure if she was sure herself. She really did not have a headache. Well, maybe she did. It was not a throbbing, hurting headache. It was more of a brain-filled heaviness in her head. She sat and watched the fish some more. Eddie walked by and given her a curious look. She knew that he wondered why she was back there after she had seemed to be in such a rush to leave.

Actually, she was avoiding her daughter now. She didn't want to talk to her any more today. She was wrong to bring the subject up in the first place. Her cell phone kept ringing. She turned it off. She knew it was Marla. Probably wanted to know how her headache was. Pia downed her third glass of wine for the afternoon and decided to go to the mall. That's what she needed to do. Go buy something. Even though she didn't need anything. She strolled through the boutiques and looked. Nothing hit her fancy. She needed to buy SOMETHING. It was what she came here for. Finally, she bought a blouse at Coldwater Creek. It was nice but she didn't need it. It was just something to buy. Two and a half hours after leaving Marla, Pia returned home. There were several messages on her answering machine and they were all from Marla.

"Mom, where are you?!!!"

Pia took the blouse out of the bag and looked at it. Maybe she shouldn't have bought it. She was not sure if she really liked it. She put it back in the bag and decided to wait and see if she really liked it tomorrow. Maybe she would just return it. She peered into the refrigerator to see if there was something she might want for supper. She was not all that hungry since she had had a fairly large lunch. Maybe an apple and some cheese. Yes, that would be good. Pia changed into some jeans and a t-shirt. Even though she dressed stylishly when she went out, Pia liked to hang out around home in comfy clothes. A little bit of soft jazz on the CD player. Yes, that would be good while reading her latest edition of Conde Nast Traveler. She carried her apple and cheese out to the deck and relaxed at the patio table. The jazz was subtle in the background.

She was halfway through the magazine and her apple and cheese when she heard a car pull into her driveway. She knew instinctively who it was but she stayed just where she was. She heard the front door slam.

"Mom, Mom, where are you?"

Pia cut another slice off her apple and a slice of cheese. She turned a page in the magazine but didn't utter a word. Marla would find her. It didn't take long. The sliding glass doors flew open and Marla stood there with her hands on her hips and fury in her face.

"Mom, what are you doing?!!"

"Uh, eating an apple and some cheese and browsing through my magazine. Hey, Marla, want to go to the Fiji Islands? They look really cool."

Pia still had not looked up at her daughter, but kept munching the apple and leafing pages. She took a sip of wine and then turned to Marla.

"Forgive me, my dear. Would you like some apple and cheese or a glass of wine?"

"No, Mother, what I want is an explanation!"

"About what?"

"Why did you rush out of the restaurant?"

"I told you. I had a headache."

Pia closed her magazine and pushed her plate aside.

"I don't believe you."

"Believe what you want to believe."

Marla paced up and down the deck and then sat in a chair across from her mother.

"Why didn't you answer your phone?"

Pia threw her hands up in the air.

"You know how I am about my cell phone. It's either not charged or I don't hear it."

"But I called you on your home phone, too."

"Oh, I forgot to look for messages."

Marla stood up.

"I'll be right back."

She came back with another wine glass. She refreshed her Mother's glass, poured herself some and settled back into the chair across from her Mother. Pia had opened the magazine again. Marla reached across the table and closed the magazine. Pia looked up at her in surprise. It was the first time since Marla's arrival that Pia had looked directly at Marla.

"What'd you do that for?"

"Mom, we have to talk."

"We talked this afternoon."

Pia started to open the "Traveler" again but Marla grabbed it away from her and then put her hand gently on her Mother's.

"Mom, I have a feeling what you were getting around to this afternoon."

Pia slouched back in her chair and closed her eyes.

"You think so?"

"Yes, I think so. Are you going to tell me more about it now?"

"There's not much more to say and I'm sorry I brought it up in the first place."

"Mother, I'm going to stay put until we have this out."

"Have what out?"

"What you are thinking."

"Good heavens, I hope you can't read my mind."

"No. I cannot read your mind. But I can read between the lines."

"And?"

Marla sat for a long time in her chair before she responded. She took a big sip of wine and then exhaled deeply.

"Mother, you started out our luncheon conversation strangely."

"I'm a strange person."

"That I will admit but then you changed tacks. You started talking about Summer."

"She's a delightful person to talk about."

Marla sighed.

"Yes, I know, Mother, and I know you have deep feelings for her."

"Yes, I do, but I have deep feelings for all the children."

Pia was almost forceful in stating this.

There was another long silence. Marla was trying to think of the right words.

"Mom, it goes beyond that. There seems to be a special bond between you and Summer."

"I had hoped it wouldn't show to anyone."

"It does and it doesn't."

"Do you think the other children think I favor Summer?"

"No. I think that they think you and Summer have a secret between you. Maybe it's a personality thing. Maybe you and Summer have a personality bond."

"Is that what you think?"

"That's what I thought until this afternoon."

"And?"

"I don't know what to think."

Marla was quiet for a little longer and then spoke. "Mother, I've got to ask you this. I've been thinking about it all day since you left after lunch. Do you think that Summer is a reincarnation of Dad?"

Pia stood up and strolled over to the edge of the deck. She looked out over the pond. Her back was to Marla and she braced her arms on the railing. She looked up at the sky and then back at the pond. The leaves were beginning to get their autumn hues. One by one, they slipped down into the pond. It made Pia think about the circles of life. The circles of life. That was a phrase that she had not thought of before. Did this prove her point or disprove it?

"I don't know but it is so weird."

Her voice was barely audible as she replied. "She is so much like him."

"Yes, Mom, I've seen that too. But she is his granddaughter."

"She didn't know him."

"That's correct but we've tried to keep his image in her mind. We have pictures of him which we have shown to her. We have talked to her about him."

Twilight was coming on. Pia stared at the sky again as the clouds turned gray and then pink and then dark. More leaves swirled into the pond. She wondered if she could read a message in the leaves in the pond like fortune-tellers read tea leaves. *But that is idiotic. People can't read fortunes in tea leaves.* But what she was thinking was idiotic, too. *People are not reincarnated. Maybe. Maybe, a squirrel is uplifted to the position of a dog. Maybe a swallow makes it to his final resting ground and comes back as an eagle. Maybe a wretched-born person is reborn as a person with fortunes. But peole are not reborn into the same family. Or are they?*

Pia turned around but did not walk back to the table. She leaned back against the railing and folded her arms. She knew that this was a symbol of rejecting someone or something and she didn't want Marla to think that that was what she was doing. She dropped her arms to her sides and started to speak but, then, couldn't help but fold them again. She lifted her face and stared right at Marla.

"Marla, I have given this a great deal of thought."

"You must have, Mom, because you usually don't come out with irrational statements."

"And you think this is an irrational thought?"

"You've got to admit that it is a bit unusual,"

"Yes, that it is. It is a very unusual thought but it didn't come overnight."

"I'm sure it didn't and that's why I wanted to talk to you."

"What have you got for rebuttal?"

Pia's arms were still clenched against her chest and she automatically tightened them a little more.

"I'm not going to rebut with you standing way over there and with your arms held tight in defense. Come sit by me again."

Pia turned back around and gazed up at the sky again. She said a short prayer to her God and then returned to the table. Slouching down in the chair, she folded her arms again.

"Mom, for Pete's sake, will you stop folding your arms tightly and relax just a little bit. We really need to talk about this calmly."

Pia unfolded her arms, placed her hands together very primly in her lap and grinned mischievously at Marla.

"Why do people use the phrase, 'for Petes sake'?"

Marla flopped her arms down on the table, a little too hard, but she didn't want her mother to see her wince.

"Who gives a damn?"

Pia smiled wryly.

"I wish you wouldn't swear."

"That's not swearing and you know it and let's get on with the subject at hand."

Pia sat up in her chair and leaned forward with her hands on the table.

"We are, in a sense. I know where that phrase comes from because of your father and I'll bet Summer knows the derivation, too."

Marla rolled her eyes and lifted her arms to the sky.

"Okay. Where does it come from?"

"It's a phrase that people use instead of saying 'for God's sake.' I guess they don't want to be blasphemous. It is rumored that a farmhand first said it when he stuck his foot with a pitchfork. He didn't want to offend the Lord. I guess onlookers picked up on it and it became a popular expression."

"That's very interesting, Mom. Here have some more wine and you can fill me in on more of your trivial facts."

"It seems to me that you are being a little bit sarcastic."

Pia accepted the glass of wine and took a healthy swig.

Marla pounded her fist on the table and then slouched back in her chair as her mother had done before.

"Okay, I did not come here to discuss trivia. I want to talk about Dad and Summer."

"And we shall, my dear."

Marla sat up straight and pulled a piece of paper out of her purse.

"When you exited the restaurant, you left this on the table."

"That's okay. You didn't have to return it to me. I have it all in my head."

"That's not the reason why I kept it. I wanted to go through it one by one."

"Suit yourself. Marla, don't you want anything to eat?"

"NO! Why did you bring up the subject of Summer inquiring about the word myth when she was two?"

Pia's face became grave. If she had acted silly before, she did not now.

"That I will explain to you after you go through the rest of the list."

Marla glanced at the list again and looked up at her mother. "What's the point about the pony?"

Pia sighed heavily.

"Summer rode that horse back and forth. Back and forth. It was strange – don't you think?"

"Did you think there was something wrong with her? She was obviously enjoying riding the horse."

Pia had a hint of a smile on her face.

"Do you remember your father mowing our grass?"

Marla turned her head to the side, stared at the pond for a moment and rotated back toward Pia. She was thinking deeply.

"I see what you mean. Dad rode his John Deere back and forth and back and forth."

Pia nodded.

"Yes, he loved that big mower. He would hop on it whether the lawn needed mowing or not. It was kind of an escape for him. No. Wait! I don't know if it was an escape from the real world or an opportunity to escape from his office and develop his novels. Either way, it was an escape. "

"And you equate that to Summer riding her horse back and forth?"

"Most definitely. And your Uncle Joe remarked about it."

"Why? What did he say?"

"He had a feeling of déjà vu when he saw Summer riding the horse. And what did Summer name her horse?"

"My Dear."

"Precisely. John Deere - My Dear."

Marla sat quietly and pondered the thought.

"But that's all coincidence, Mom. It's just something that you and Uncle Joe put into it. Maybe you wanted to see Dad in Summer."

"That could be. Excuse me for a minute. I've got to use the ladies room."

Marla studied the notes again and then went in to get another bottle of wine. She was going to get to the bottom of this if it took all the wine that her mother had. She was just going to sit and keep interrogating. She incidentally picked up a box of crackers from the pantry.

Pia was sitting back on the deck when Marla returned and uncorked the second bottle of wine.

"Marla, you're going to get us drunk! But I'm glad to see that you got yourself something to eat."

"Maybe I need to get drunk."

Marla poured them both a glass of wine and helped herself to a handful of crackers.

"Next point. Summer taking Latin in high school."

"I just thought it unusual. Latin is very seldom taught any more. Very few students want to study a dead language."

"You know as well as I do that Latin is not a dead language."

"That's why I brought it up. Your father was vehement that Latin was not a dead language and that there was much to be gained by studying it. "

"Well, Mom, that's probably the environment that Summer was raised in. You were very instrumental in teaching her that money is not a goal. Money will come to you if you pursue your own goals. Learning is all important to achieve goals. The more you learn, the more you will achieve."

"You are very deep."

"No. You and Dad were very deep. You taught Eric and me a lot."

"We tried."

"Ah, but you did and it was passed down to my children and Eric's children."

Pia considered this for a while. It was indeed a compliment and made sense. Hugh had always encouraged his children to explore the world. It didn't matter whether it was a bird feather on the sidewalk or the meaning of a word or where Timbuktu was located. *And the school projects...oh, my god, the school projects* . Marla and Eric would approach him and tell him that they had a project. Hugh would sit them down and say, "What are you most interested in?"

There were very interesting projects- no little volcanoes for them. Hugh even took Eric on a geologic dig. Not in Egypt or Turkey but a local dig that gave Eric a very good experience, enriched his knowledge and gave him an A+ on his science project. And it passed on to Noel and Jade and Summer. Pia reminisced as long as she could and then turned toward Marla.

"Okay, I'll accept that. What's next?"

"Summer studying journalism in college."

"Yes, she did. Your father also took journalism classes but he really wanted to be a writer just like Summer."

At this point, Pia turned her chair to watch the pond again. It was now completely dark but the moonlight glowed off the shimmering waters of the pond. She was on the verge of tears and didn't want Marla to see them. Again, Hugh's words appeared in her head. *I wish you didn't have to work. Someday I'll be able to support us with my novels.*

Marla tried to pretend that her mother had not turned away and addressed her as though she was talking directly to her mother.

"Mother, this is a genetics strain. And it comes from both you and Dad. Of course, Dad had a way with words. That was his specialty and his career. You, also, are quite good with words. You are a fabulous punster. A love of language has been installed in Summer. Either by genetics or environment. Don't you see that?"

Pia tried to inconspicuously wipe away a tear that had trickled down her cheek. She still wouldn't turn to Marla. Her voice was very low.

"Yes, it could be attributed to that. I will concede but I'm not totally convinced."

"What's it going to take to convince you?"

Marla poured another glass of wine for herself and then, as an afterthought, poured some for Pia. She was becoming more and more confused, but was determined to go on.

Pia stood pat where she was . She had again assumed the position of folded arms.

"I'll tell you later. Go ahead with the next point."

"Scotch."

"Ah, yes. Why does Summer like Scotch?"

"Just 'cuz she likes it."

"Do you like it?"

"Hell, no!"

"Do I like it?"

"Not that I know of."

"DO YOU know anybody who likes Scotch except for Summer?"

"No."

"So this is not a case of environment. Summer likes Scotch. Her grandfather liked Scotch."

"Well, Mom, maybe this is a case of genetics."

Pia turned and looked back at Marla.

"For goodness sake, there are many things that can be attributed to genetics. Blue eyes versus brown eyes. Big bones versus a small frame. The way your hair swirls at the crown of your head. Et cetera, et cetera. I've never heard of anyone acquiring a taste for Scotch through genetics."

Marla threw up her arms .

"So what! Maybe it's just a quirky thing that Summer developed. You know how all of us pick up on quirky things when we are young."

"It just seems odd to me."

"Yes, I'll admit it is odd but it is just a coincidence that Summer likes Scotch and so did Dad."

"Okay, I'll go along with that just to appease you."

"I don't need to be appeased. Let's go on."

Marla sighed, took a sip of wine and shoved another cracker in her mouth.

"It's about Summer cheating."

Pia burst out laughing and couldn't stop. When she had calmed down a little, she remarked. "Marla, you shouldn't talk with food in your mouth."

"That's not what you were laughing at, Mom."

"So you know this point as well as I do. Hugh cheated all the time just in the same way that Summer does. He didn't cheat at important things in life like his contracts or dealings with people. He cheated at silly things like friendly games. And everyone knew and everyone laughed at him and with him. Summer gets away with it, too. It's because everyone loves her and they know that she does not mean any harm. Her personality is so much like Hugh's in that way."

Marla couldn't help but smile a little. She had very strong memories in that area. "Yeah, Mom, I remember when he would go golfing with his buddies and they would all come back to our house. They all told tall tales about the day but they were all adamant that Daddy had cheated. Either replacing his ball or putting the wrong score down on his card. And it apparently didn't bother anyone because they all wanted to play golf with him again. And he cheated in little childhood games with me. Did you know that?"

"Of course I knew that. Sometimes he cheated to let you win and sometimes he cheated to make you lose. It was all done as a learning experience for you."

Marla looked somber again.

"Did he ever cheat on you?"

"Not that I know of, dear. I'm ninety-nine percent sure he didn't. We just got along too well. Anyhow, that wasn't his brand of cheating."

"Why do you say ninety-nine percent sure?"

"Honey, you can't be one hundred percent sure of anything in this world. There's always a chance of miscalculation."

"Maybe you've miscalculated on this thing we are talking about."

"Oh, that could be a very strong possibility. I'm not saying that this is for real. I'm saying what I've thought about. It's been on my mind for many years now."

"And you've never mentioned it to anyone before?"

"How could I? It's absurd, isn't it?"

"Yes."

Marla turned to face the pond. The moonlight was still strong upon it. She was trying to think of something profound to say. Her mind was completely boggled. Was her mother crazy? Or was she seeing something that they all should have caught on to? *Yes, I have noticed a slight similarity between my daughter and my father, but I accepted that as genetics, just as you'd think about your child - 'isn't that cute? It's just like her grandfather used to do.' And that's all the thought you put into it.* But apparently her mother had put a lot more thought into it. A LOT more thought. Was she obsessing? Was she just trying to have Hugh back if even through Summer? Well, it is obvious that children live through their parents and grandparents, but not through reincarnation. It is the environment they were raised in or the genes that were passed down to them. The point that struck Marla most was the riding of the pony. She remembered her father going back and forth across the yard on his riding lawn mower. He was in a trance just as Summer had been when riding her pony. Of course, the Scotch issue made no sense at all. Nobody drank Scotch except Summer. And her grandfather. She kept going through all the points in her mind. Most of them she could reconcile. But her mother was convincing, too. This was just too weird! She stared at the pond some more.

Marla became transfixed by the pond. The moonlight played images on the smooth water. The leaves were twisting and turning and forming more images. She saw her father's face. She saw Summer's face. They were separate and then merged together. Marla had never thought that Summer had a striking resemblance to her grandfather but the faces melted into one. It was an illusion. It had to be an illusion! Maybe she had too much wine and it was affecting her sanity. Marla picked up the wine bottle and gazed at the label. It seemed innocuous enough. She turned to the pond again. The images were fainter but still there. She shook her head. It didn't change anything. It was like one of those crazy e-mails you received. An optical illusion. Nothing more. Nothing less. Marla wanted to run down to the pond and stir up the leaves but she was spellbound. *Oh! It is not true. It can't be. Or could it be? Mom does have some valid points. But that's all coincidence. Is there such a thing as coincidence?*

"Mom, where's your dictionary?"

"On my desk. Why?"

"There's just something I want to look up."

"Go ahead."

As Marla expected, the dictionary was at the front of her mother's desk. She quickly flipped the pages to find C-O-I.

Coincidence: 1. the fact or condition of coinciding; correspondence. 2. A remarkable concurrence of events, ideas, etc., apparently by mere chance.

Marla considered this and moved her finger up the page.

Coincide: 1. To have the same dimensions and position in space; be in the same place. 2. To occur at the same time or for the same time span. 3. To agree exactly; accord.

Yes, that is what coincidence is, but it's not just happenstance like I thought. The first definition of coincide really held her thoughts. *"To have the same dimensions and position in space; be in the same place." Could this explain reincarnation? To be in the same space.* The faces in the pond were in the same space. One was her father and one her daughter. They converged into one. Marla was dizzy. She steadied herself on the edge of the desk and closed her eyes. Her thoughts were whirling just like the leaves on the pond. All she saw was yellow and gold and brown going circling in her head. She slowly lowered herself into the chair and opened her eyes. The first thing she saw was the thesaurus. Why? She didn't know, but she picked it up and chased down another word. The synonyms for reincarnate were repeat, do again, redo, duplicate, renew, revive and many more of the same genre.

Marla stood up and walked slowly back to the deck. There were no faces on the pond. Her mother was still sitting at the table. She apparently had picked up her magazine again and was leafing through it. Marla sat down across from Pia and looked at the pond. Then the moon. Then the stars. No faces anywhere. Not even the man in the moon. She put the palms of her hands to her eyes and rubbed them. She was tired. So very tired.

Pia let her daughter be silent. She knew what must be going through Marla's head. The reason she had left the restaurant with a faked headache was because she couldn't go through with it. But her daughter had persisted so she had no choice. She wished she had never brought it up. This time she was beginning to get a real headache. It had been wrong of her. It was a terrible weight to put on her daughter. And her daughter might just think that she was plain crazy. She'd have to deal with either of these facts. There was one more thing she had to point out to Marla and she really didn't know if she wanted to.

She gazed at Marla's silhouette. She was such a beautiful girl and Pia was so fond of her. Why did she put this abstruse idea on her? Marla would go home and tell Craig. He would insist that Pia be put into a loony bin. It was probably justifiable. But it had let a little steam out of Pia to let it go to Marla.

Marla was no longer staring at the pond. She had dropped her elbows to her knees and buried her face in her hands. Pia had no idea what Marla was thinking now. *Oh my God! What have I done?*

She smiled within herself. *I should change that to 'For Pete's sake!'*
What have I done?

Marla lifted her head out of her hands and turned back to her
mother and stared straight at her.

"Okay, Mom, you skipped a point. You said you would get back
to it."

Pia knew what she was talking about but didn't know if she
really wanted to reveal it.

"What's that?"

"You brought up the incident when Summer celebrated her
second birthday. After everyone had left except you, she asked me
what the word myth meant. I almost don't want to know now what
your insinuations are on this. You and I both know a fact that ties
the word myth to Summer. I didn't put it together until just now.
Okay. Tell me! How does this tie to Dad?"

Pia shivered but not from the dropping temperature.

"Are you cold, Mom? You want me to get you a sweater?"

"No, dear, because we are going inside anyway. I have something
to show you."

Marla was puzzled but also inquisitive. She watched her mother
get up slowly, very slowly, from her chair and followed her into the
house. Pia led Marla to the bedroom and instructed her to sit on the
bed. Pia knelt down on the floor and opened the file cabinet. She
knew exactly where to reach for the hanging folder. She had pulled
it out many, many time in the past few years. Especially in the past
year. Carefully, she handed the folder to Marla. She didn't want to
drop any of the papers in them and get them mixed up.

Marla took the folder and opened the olive green leaf. She looked
at the first page and gasped. Her hand flew to her mouth. She was
stunned and could not say anything. Pia readjusted her position. She
remained on the floor but pulled her legs up to her chest. She put
her head down on her knees. She was in a turmoil as she was sure
her daughter was too. But she had had this turmoil for a long time
while her daughter hadn't had a clue.

Pia was the first to speak.

"Marla, as far as you know, did Summer ever come and look in this file cabinet?"

"I don't know if she even knew it existed. I certainly didn't know."

"That's what I thought. But there is that possibility."

"Yes, like you said, you can't be one hundred percent sure."

"But that would mean she was cheating. Not playful cheating but real cheating."

Marla was crying now.

"I don't believe that my daughter would indulge in that type of cheating. And that means that your theory is more considerable. Oh, my God!"

Pia grinned.

"You mean, 'for Pete's sake.'"

Marla had to laugh. Her mother could always make her feel better.

"Yes, Mother, for Pete's sake. But I do think that God has something to do with this."

Pia was solemn.

"Depending on whose God you are talking about."

"You have done a little research into this haven't you?"

"I had to."

Marla slowly read the first page again. It was the letter addressed to Hugh's agent. The letter that all writers have to write. The letter that explains the material. Well, Hugh didn't actually have to write the letter. He already had an agent who went through his publisher. But he preferred to do it this way, just as he had many, many times in the past. Pia thought that he kept it humble as though he was just a "starting –out" writer.

"For centuries, peoples of the world have believed in myths, legends and religions. Did it help them through their daily drudgery or hold them captive – enslaved to prevailing ideas? That is the theme of my newest novel."

Marla was breathing heavily and trying to restrain tears.

"That's what Summer wrote about! That's the book she wrote and is nominated for - for the Nobel Prize! I've got to call her!"

Pia thought over the idea. Maybe it was the best way to go at this time. She walked out of the bedroom and then came back without saying a word to Marla. She placed the cordless phone in Marla's hand. Tears were welling in Marla's eyes but she tried to hide them. She kept wiping them away as they started to drip down her cheek. She started to dial Summer's number. Pia looked away.

"Uh, Mom, can you hand me a Kleenex?"

Pia walked over to the dresser and put the box of Kleenex down next to Marla. She had a feeling that her daughter was going to need more than one tissue. Marla blew her nose and stared at the phone while Pia sat down on the edge of the bed. Marla kept staring at the phone. Pia patted her shoulder.

"Go ahead, honey. It's going to clear up a few things for us both."

"I can't."

Marla sniffled.

"Why can't you?"

Marla managed a smile.

"I can't remember Summer's number."

Pia laughed.

"Of course you do. We both call it all the time."

"But I can't remember right now. I've got a mental block."

Pia gave her the phone number and left the room. She wasn't sure that she wanted to hear the conversation. But she did stay close enough to the bedroom door so that she could hear talking-not the exact conversation but just the low murmur of Marla's voice.

The voices stopped and Pia came back into the bedroom.

"So what did she say?"

"She didn't answer. Apparently she wasn't home . I left a message on her answering machine."

"What did you say?"

"Only to call me. Mom, I am so tired and confused."

"I know, my dear. Why don't you lie down on my bed and get some sleep. I'll lie down on my sofa. We are both tired and confused. Let's get some sleep"

"I gotta call Craig and tell him I'm staying here."

"Yes, do that and go to bed. I'll be on the sofa."

Pia started to leave the room and then hesitated. She turned back to Marla.

"Marla, there's just one more thing I have to tell you."

Marla looked up with her reddened eyes.

"And what is that?"

"Did I ever tell you what your father's last words were?"

"No. I guess 'good-bye' or 'I love you or' something like that."

"No. The last thing he said was 'One child.'"

Marla looked up in surprise.

"What does that mean?"

"Marla, my dear, I never figured it out until a few days ago. I heard it on the radio and realized what he was trying to say."

"You heard it on the radio! My father's last words?!"

"Well, actually, I heard a song. A song that explains the reason he said that."

"Which was?" Marla sunk into the pillow.

Pia approached the bed and grabbed her daughter's hand. "Marla, it was called 'And When I Die,' by Blood Sweat and Tears.

Pia crooned in her poor singing voice, "There'll be one child born to carry on."

Marla withdrew her hands from her mother's and covered her eyes.

"Oh, my God!"

"You mean, 'for Pete's sake!'"

Marla sat up and hugged her Mother.

"Yes, Mom."

Pia paused and took a deep breath. She gently stroked her daughter's hair back from her face.

"There is one thing that I read in my research about people who are supposedly reincarnated. There is a term called mediumistic possession. The reincarnated person has no recollection of a past life. However, they exhibit the past person in various ways, such as a familiar word or action."

Marla yawned.

"Such as a myth or a John Deere or Scotch."

"Okay, Marla, let's get some sleep if we can. Sweet dreams, my lovely girl."

Marla slumped down again.

"I'll try, Mom. I'll really try."

Pia got up and fetched a blanket and pillow to take to the sofa and thought to herself. *Peaceful dreams, Pia and Marla. Peaceful dreams.*

Marla left bright and early in the morning. It was too bright and early because she had not gotten very much sleep. She did sleep well but it was the wee hours of the morning when she went to sleep. She had been up very, very late with her mother and they had drunk a bunch of wine but it was drunk slowly enough so that neither one of them felt intoxicated. Probably they were too dazed by all the facts to get intoxicated. There was too much thinking and absorbing to do.

Pia was still asleep on the sofa when Marla left. She tiptoed through the living room and closed the door. It looked like her mother was sleeping peacefully for she was snoring a bit. Of course, that could have been due to the wine. Craig had left for work when Marla arrived home. She walked the empty rooms of the house, especially stopping in Summer's room. What was the truth?

18.

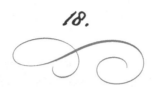

Whatever Marla had thought, Pia had not slept peacefully. She tossed and turned on the sofa. She felt that she was asleep but she thought she was awake. She heard a voice. It was not Marla's voice. It was a man's voice and she knew it well.

"Pia. Noetic! You will find the answer. Pia. Noetic! Do not forget the word."

Pia awoke in a cold sweat. She was a little disorientated and then she remembered. Marla had spent the night in her bed and she had slept on the sofa. She tiptoed into the bedroom. Marla was gone and the bed had been made up. Wasn't that nice of Marla. She had raised a good girl! And then her mind wandered back to her dream. She sat down at the computer and googled.

"Noetic: derived from the Greek _nous_ for which there is no exact equivalent in English. Noetic refers to 'inner feeling' – a kind of intuitive consciousness. A direct and immediate access to knowledge beyond what is available to our normal senses and the power of reason." Pia sunk into her chair and thought about this for a long time. She recalled the conversation with her daughter last night. Suddenly, she bolted up from her chair.

"One Child Born!," she screamed to an empty house. After rifling through numerous papers on her desk, she found what it was she was looking for. According to some Buddhist thinking, at the death of one personality, a new one comes into being, much as the flame of a dying candle can serve to light the flame of another.

Another word of that night was not mentioned by Pia or Marla. They simply could not ask Summer about it. Summer had returned Marla's call but Marla said she couldn't remember why she had called. It must not have been important, she explained. The night's discussion remained a secret between Pia and Marla and they didn't talk about it although it was constantly on their minds. Marla didn't even tell Craig even though she hesitated in her conversations with him as though to tell the whole implications. She didn't know what to say to Summer. Did she cheat and copy files from her grandfather. Or was she a reincarnation of her grandfather? Was another candle lit?

The word noetic preyed on Pia's mind. "A kind of intuitive consciousness. A direct and immediate access to knowledge beyond what is available to our normal senses and the power of reason." It was Hugh's voice that prompted her to look up noetic science. Was he trying to communicate with her? Was he trying to tell her to trust her instincts? Was he trying to tell her that he lives again in Summer? Or was he just communicating with her. AND Summer. *These things that coincide might not be reincarnation but Hugh's communication with us. Communication with me. Communication with Summer. Intuitive consciousness. Is that what Summer had when she rode the horse, My Dear, around and around the yard? Is that what Summer has when she recognized Stan at her birthday party? Is that had when she asked her Mommy what the meaning of myth was? Was that, was that , was that! Did Summer have an intuitive consciousness? Did she have direct and immediate access to knowledge that is beyond our human senses?*

19.

Christmas after Sweden was over. Pia had not brought up the subject and neither had Marla. Neither one of them wanted to think that Summer had copied Hugh's files. But, even if she had, what did it matter? She had won the Nobel Prize for her grandfather. But Pia remained puzzled about it. She really didn't think that Summer knew about the file. It was something that she had kept hidden away behind the house records and insurance records and tax records. Why in the world would Summer find them or even search for them? She had been interested in Hugh's writings and had read all of his books. But why would she look for anything else? Pia was so confused. On one hand, if Summer had seen the file and written a book on it and won the Nobel Prize for it, who cares? She was carrying on for Hugh. But was it cheating to take someone else's partial manuscript and make a prize-winning book out of it?

Marla also paced her floors and wondered the same thoughts. Craig would find her wandering in the middle of the night as she strolled through the house. Or, maybe, just huddled in a blanket on the living room sofa. He would ask her what was wrong. She couldn't offer an explanation. This was a secret between her mother and her. Craig would think them both crazy.

Pia could take it no longer. She had to talk to Marla seriously again. She put her hand on the phone and hesitated. To phone or not to phone, – that was the question. The question was resolved when the phone rang of it's own accord. It was Marla.

"Mom, I've been thinking...."

"And so have I, my dear. Wanna do lunch tomorrow?"

"Exactly what I was thinking. About noon tomorrow at the aquarium place?"

"Suits me. I really need to talk to you."

"Ditto. See you on the morrow."

They were both exactly on time and met in the foyer. After being seated, they stared at each other for a long time and then burst out laughing. Their server, who happened to be Eddie again, took their drink orders and left them with the menus to peruse.

Pia opened her menu and started to scan it when Marla spoke up. "Mom, I seriously don't think that Summer knew about Dad's files."

Pia closed her menu and looked straight into Marla's eyes.

" I don't think so either and I'll explain to you why but you'll probably think I am crazy again or still crazy."

Eddie arrived with a carafe of wine and two glasses. The women remained quiet while Eddie ceremoniously poured each of them a glass of Chardonnay.

"Are you ladies ready to order yet?"

"Not quite yet, Eddie. We haven't even looked at the menu. Come back a in a few."

Pia and Marla smiled at him with gracious grins as if to dismiss him. He nodded and walked away.

"Okay, Marla, why don't you think that Summer saw the files?"

"First of all, if she had seen them, she would have come to one of us. She would have said 'Look at this stuff. It's fascinating!' If she wanted to expand on it and finish the work, she would have asked for your permission."

"*But,* Marla, what if she *was* poking around or peeking? What if she thought that if she had found the files because of snooping, we would accuse her of wrongdoing?"

"No, I disagree."

Marla was adamant.

" We all know that Summer cheats on trivial stuff and makes people laugh but she wouldn't cheat on something as important as this. I could be wrong, but I absolutely trust my little ray of sunshine, my Summer."

Pia's eyes sparkled into the widest manifest of approval that her face could muster. She nodded her head up and down vigorously.

" I'm completely on your side, my dear. That's why I had to talk to you. I have some new ideas. Well, some new and some old. I'm kind of tossed up with them."

"Well, spring them on me!"

"Let's look at the menu and order first. Then we can get down to specifics without Eddie bothering us."

Eddie, as a good server, had been watching to see when the ladies would be ready to order. He saw them reading and then close the menus and set them aside. He strolled by leisurely as though by accident.

"Are you ready for something delicious now?"

Pia grinned at him.

"Yes, I am. How about the pork tenderloin with pineapple curry chutney?"

"Excellent choice. And you, ma'am?"

He turned toward Marla.

"I'll have the grouper cheeks."

"Another excellent choice. They were just flown in today and are fresh and delightful."

Eddie accepted the menus proffered to him and walked off. He had a feeling he was in for a pretty decent tip.

"Mom, you didn't order fish today and you are not staring at the fish."

"Nope. I don't need any more brain food, either visually or sensually."

"And that's why I ordered the grouper. I just have a feeling that I am going to have to use my brain a lot during this conversation with you."

Pia smiled wryly.

"Maybe, maybe not. How open is your brain?"

"With you, I'm not always sure. You can be so conservative in some matters but then, you'll be off-the-wall."

"Fair enough. What I have to say to you today might be considered off-the-wall."

"I'm game, but only because you look a lot more relaxed than you did when we last met at this restaurant."

"Okay, ready for this?"

Pia described to Marla the vision that she had on the evening that Marla had spent the night after viewing Hugh's myth manuscript. She explained the definition of noetics and the implications.

"Wow!"

It was the only word that could come out of Marla's mouth. She didn't know what else to say. Luckily, Eddie reappeared with their entrees.

Marla took a bite of her grouper. She chewed it carefully and looked at her mother.

"I really need this brain food now. I really have a lot to ask and say now and I don't know what comes first."

"Say the first thing that comes to your mind... as long as it's not blasphemous or evil."

"The first thing that comes to my mind is transcendency."

"Ah, yes, I have thought of that too because it does follow in the path of noetics , doesn't it."

"From what you have told me – yes. But who has transcended? Has Summer transcended and gotten knowledge from her grandfather? Or have you transcended and communicated with my father? Or was my father in such a state of transcendency when he died that he was able to communicate with you and/or Summer?"

Pia thought about the question for a long time. She took a bite of her pork and chewed. She sipped her wine. Marla waited patiently and then asked another question.

"Mom, does this mean you have dismissed the idea of reincarnation?"

Pia rubbed her temples.

"My brain is overloaded and also feels light-headed. Isn't that an oxymoron? I think about one thing and weigh it. I think about the other thing and weigh it. They all seem to either conflict or coincide. To answer your question. No, I have not given up the idea of reincarnation. As you must know, I did a lot of investigation about reincarnation. I don't make a statement that seriously without some really serious thought."

"I know that, Mom. You are a level-headed woman and think things out before you express an opinion. That's why I wondered about you the first time you hinted about reincarnation."

For the first time that day, Pia stared at the aquarium fish. She didn't turn to Marla again as she spoke but kept staring at the fish.

"Yes, I did do a lot of researching. There are various religions, sects, cults, et cetera, et cetera that do believe in reincarnation. Of course, there also those who just believe that when you die, that's it. You are just fodder for the soil. And then there are the believers in being with a heavenly God forever. You don't come back to Earth. You just become an angel and float among the clouds. Of course, I am oversimplifying here."

Marla didn't try to break her mother's concentration or try to distract her from the fish. She just asked very quietly, "And what do you think, Mom?"

"I don't know. It is all very confusing. I expect that Summer would say that when we die, we die. That's it. There is no memory and no soul to fly off to parts unknown. She would believe that a concept of heaven and hell or reincarnation is a myth - a myth that was conceived so that people would not fear dying. Or perhaps a myth that people could interpret that heaven was a place where they did not simply abandon life but continued it in another dimension."

"What do you think, GrandPi?"

Pia was startled by the question. Not exactly by the question but the way it was addressed. She turned her attention away from the fish and stared at Marla.

"Why did you call me GrandPi?"

"I really don't know. It's funny I said that and it's funny you noticed. I always call you Mom to your face. The children call you GrandPi. However, I do refer to you as GrandPi when we are talking about you behind your back. "

Pia laughed.

"Maybe you are talking for or defending your daughter."

"I don't think so. I have my own thoughts which are often a lot different than hers. But maybe I was speaking for her subconsciously."

Pia kept her eyes on Marla. "I'll accept that explanation and get back to it later. But, I'll get on with my thoughts and try to answer your question. I prefer not to think that people just plain die where there is nothingness. If that is true, that's okay, too. What's the loss? You are gone. You are buried. You are done with. There is nothing to think about. There is nothing to dwell on. Everything previous in your life is simply erased. That's it. Nada. Nothing. Yes, your friends and family will mourn your death but that's their problem. To you it means nothing.

"The possibility of Heaven and being an angel is cute. I really enjoy the television shows and movies that show people coming back to earth as angels and helping out people in need. I would love to do that. I can think of a thousand people I would love to come back and visit and help straighten out their lives. Maybe that's the theory that I want to believe in most. However, the idea of reincarnation fascinates me more. There are religions that believe a person can come back as anything – be it animal, vegetable or mineral. You could come back as a cat or a blade of grass or a grain of salt.

"Most people, when referring to reincarnation, refer to some elegant animal. 'I'd like to come back as a swan. I'd like to come back as a cheetah. I'd like to come back as a dolphin.' I've considered this realm of thought and laugh to myself. Now, Marla, consider this. What would you think if you came back as a rat or a cockroach?"

"I'd think that my God was punishing me."

"Why?"

"Because they are both nasty ugly creatures."

"Aha! They are ugly nasty creatures to you but who knows what goes on in their little minds. Do they think of themselves as being ugly and nasty? They might be trying to raise a happy little family and live a happy life foraging. And then some big ugly monster comes along and ends their life. So they die and then come back reincarnated as something else. A swan, a cheetah, a dolphin. Who knows? Maybe they believe in reincarnation too. Maybe they say that they'd like to come back as a swan or cheetah or dolphin."

"Mom, rats and cockroaches don't have brains like that."

"How do you know?"

"I don't know. I do think that dolphins and dogs and cats and monkeys might have brains that function close to ours but not rats and cockroaches."

"We could talk about this supposition for a long time but I want to get to another aspect of reincarnation. Some religions believe that you come back as another human. You come back to improve upon what you did in a former life. A math teacher might come back with new technological abilities that could benefit mankind. A family practitioner might come back as a scientist and find a cure for cancer. A garage mechanic might come back and find a way to use alternate fuels more efficiently. We all know we need improvement and we might not achieve it in our lifetime But we can come back and improve ourselves. Perhaps working for science or for equality or for peace on earth. It might not happen in one reincarnation but it could happen in several reincarnations. You take one baby step at a time until you reach perfection."

"And where does Mother Teresa fit into this scheme, Mom?"

"I think that Mother Teresa has gone through many, many reincarnations and she is now safely situated next to the throne of God."

"But Mother Teresa was a very humble person. Suppose she didn't think she was perfect enough."

"That's a very good topic, Marla. I hadn't thought about that angle. What if a saintly person like Mother Teresa thinks she needs improvement? Would she ask the Gods to send her back so she could become even more perfect? Would she become transcendent or is she already transcendent. Of course, Mother Teresa was Catholic and believed in only one God whom she could not transcend. But what about the ancient religions that had many Gods? Some of the Caesars believed that they were Gods or destined to be Gods. Did they believe that they could transcend Jupiter? What do you think?"

"Mom, those are really good points. However, I have a question about this theory. Say that people do come back as another person who is an improved upon model. The family practitioner comes back as a scientist and discovers a cure for cancer. During his lifetime, he has seen so many people die from cancer and he feels helpless. He wishes he could do more but he's limited in his training and ability. He's reincarnated as a person who has the capability to find *the cure*. That's wonderful. It's something that he has always dreamed of. He has excelled in his career. He has surpassed his abilities. I guess he never knows that, at one time, he was a Podunk doctor in a Podunk town. Is that right?"

"I do think you are right on that. For the most part, people do not know they have been reincarnated although a lot of field studies have proven differently. Shirley McLaine is a good example and what about the story of Bridey Murphey, to only mention a couple. Some people's stories are hoaxes but some seem to be interesting and worth giving a thought to."

"I have another salient point. You claim that a reincarnated person is put back into our society to improve on himself. To improve on himself - 'how?' Does Charles Manson come back to improve on his life of killing? Was Ted Bundy a reincarnation of Jack the Ripper? Is there transcendency to the devil as well as to a God?"

"If you believe in a devil. I personally don't. Just like cold is the absence of heat and dark is the absence of light, evil is the absence of holiness or goodness. I prefer to think that Charles Manson would be reincarnated a little at a time and eventually become someone like Father Damian."

"You think the devil is a myth but you still believe in reincarnation." Marla stated this very matter- of- factly.

"It makes sense to me. But I like believing in the myths if they are myths that satisfy my thinking. In her book, Summer debunks a lot of myths she but also puts forth an explanation of why people believe them. Sometimes people need myths. They keep you on an even keel when the rest of the world is topsy-turvy. Religions believe in a God of some sort. People pray to their God to get them through unhappy circumstances. Is there a God? I don't know for sure but I believe in a God. You have to think that somebody or something is controlling the universe. There is a force that develops the world. Is it a God or is it Mother Nature or something else? If it is Mother Nature, then, aha! God is a woman."

Pia laughed and clapped her hands together.

Marla also laughed and then stared hard at her mother.

"So do you really believe in reincarnation or not?"

Pia sighed.

"My dear, that is a difficult question to answer. My brain sometimes tells me no but my heart tells me yes. Do I believe that Summer is a reincarnation of Hugh? Do I believe that because I want my Hugh back? And because I would do anything I could to bring him back, do I believe he is reincarnated in Summer? That's a toughie! But there are just so many similarities. You've seen it yourself."

"After you revealed things to me, yes, I did see them. I might have seen some myself and said, 'Isn't that cute. She's just like her grandfather.' What really knocked me for a loop was seeing the manuscript."

"The one that your father had started before he died."

"Yes."

"Me, too. I didn't know what to think. I was sure that Summer had never seen it. And I was the only person who ever knew about it."

Time had passed by quickly. They had finished the carafe of wine and Eddie left the bill on the table. The women agreed that they ought to leave and free the booth for someone else. However, there was so much more to be deliberated.

"Marla, have you discussed any of this with Craig?"

"No, I have not. I wanted to. I would pace and pause and act like I was going to talk to him about something and then I would change my mind."

"Do you think we should include him? He is Summer's father. Should we talk to Eric, also?"

" I want to talk to Craig about this. It's tormenting me. I should talk to my husband about something that's tormenting me, don't you think?"

"That's what makes up a good marriage."

"But I'm scared to. What if he thinks I've gone completely overboard? What if he tells Summer about this? I just don't know about this, Mom."

"Would you like me to talk with him privately ? Tell him what I think? Then, the only person he will think is crazy is me. He probably thinks that about me anyway. You don't have to be involved."

"Mom, Craig doesn't think you are crazy. Sometimes a little eccentric but not crazy. In fact, he enjoys your views about a lot of subjects. I'm going to dive off a deep end."

Marla took a deep breath, looked at the fish for a moment and then turned her face back to her mother's.

"Mom, come have dinner with us tonight and we'll confide in him."

"Are you sure, Marla?"

"Positively. He is Summer's father and he needs to know what I'm thinking about her."

"Tonight?"

"Yes, tonight, because I have made up my mind to tell him. I don't want to back out and I want my Mommy with me."

"What about Eric?"

"No, let's leave Eric out for the time being. Just you and me and Craig. "

"Okay. But don't go to any trouble for dinner. My gosh, we've had quite a big lunch here. Just get a pizza or I can stop on my way and pick up some tacos or burgers."

"Don't worry about that, Mom. We better get out of here before they think we are part of the staff and make us wash dishes."

20.

Arriving home, Pia took off her jacket and lay down on her bed. She intended to take a short nap before going over to have dinner with Marla and Craig. Her mind wouldn't let her sleep. This was going to be tricky and Marla knew it too. First of all, why hadn't they disclosed their thoughts to Craig earlier. After all, Summer was his daughter too. Would he think that they were excluding him? Would he think that they were crazy? Would he accept or be in denial of what they *might be* imagining? Craig had known Hugh for a short time and admired him. Did he know enough about Hugh to see these traits in Summer? So many emotions conflicted in Pia's head.

She was so tired. She was not tired from the day so far but from everything that had been running through her head for so long. She wanted to sleep, sleep, sleep. Finally she did doze off for a while and felt refreshed when she awoke. She looked at the clock and realized she had dozed (or slept) longer than she had anticipated.

It was almost time to go over to Marla's house for dinner. She had planned to make a dessert but there was not time for that now. A fresh green salad. That would be good with pizza. She pulled some greens out of the 'frig and looked around the refrigerator and pantry to find additives. Some sliced green olives and a few green onions. And, aha! she found a can of artichoke hearts in the pantry. That would make a good salad with pizza. She whipped up a vinaigrette dressing to go with the salad. Just good olive oil and balsamic with some mustard and a few herbs. She washed her face and put on fresh make-up and was off in her car.

"Thank you, Mom, for the salad. You didn't have to do that."

"I know but I couldn't come over here empty handed. I was going to make a dessert but didn't have the time."

She looked at Marla with a hint of guiltiness.

"I took a little nap and it lasted longer than I thought it would. Anyway, I thought a salad would be good with pizza."

Marla laughed.

"Actually, Mom, we are not having pizza. When Craig found out that you were coming over for dinner, he wanted to make something special. He has fixed braciolle and is cooking it over the grill. I was just putting the finishing touches on a marinara sauce and getting ready to make a salad. You saved me the time. All I have to do now is boil some pasta . What would you prefer? Shells, linguine, or fettuccine?"

"I think I would like linguine."

"Comin' up. Can I get you something to drink. Mom?"

"Not just yet. I'll just sit here and watch you stare at a pot of water ready to boil."

"But you know that watched water never boils."

"Yes it does. You just have to be patient."

At that point, Craig walked in with a flourish. He bowed deeply and then ran over to give Pia a hug.

"Welcome to my house, GrandPi. You are one of my favorite women!"

Pia gave him a sly smile.

"Uh huh? One of your favorites? And who might the others be?"

Craig would not be undone. He pointed to Marla.

"Now, she has to be a favorite. Thanks to you that she is around. And there are Summer and Jade."

Craig poised in thought. He walked up to Marla's back and put his arms around her. Then, with a wink, he said, "And there's my curvaceous secretary and my sexy dental hygienist and my all-too-beautiful barber."

Marla dug her elbow into his ribs and he gave her a little kiss on the cheek.

Pia enjoyed this scene and thought back to her years with Hugh. *Oh to have them again!*

"So when is dinner going to be ready? I'm starving!"

"Mom, you had a big lunch. But it will be ready soon. I'm just waiting for the water to boil. How's your end doing, Craig?"

"I'm ready to bring 'em in. Got the sauce ready?"

"Ready and waiting."

Dinner was delightful and delicious. The three of them discussed the events of the past week, the stock market, politics and everything else under the sun except the topic that Pia and Marla were avoiding. Pia mopped up the last of Marla's hearty marinara with garlic bread. She felt like she was going to explode.

"Oh, Marla and Craig, that was so sumptuous. I couldn't even swallow a thin mint now."

"It's lucky that I don't have any thin mints. However, I do have a Sara Lee cheesecake. Since you didn't bring dessert, I had to forage around in my freezer."

"Marla, I'm full!"

"Just a teeny slice and we'll have some amaretto and coffee."

Everyone was settled back in their chairs and looked relaxed, but there was tension in the air. Craig noticed it.

"What's up with you ladies? The dinner was great. The company was great. The conversation was great. But, yet, I noticed something else was going on. You gonna tell me?"

Pia and Marla gave each other surreptitious looks. Pia swished the coffee around in her cup and looked seriously at Craig.

"I don't know how to approach this but I want to explain something to you."

She fidgeted for a moment and then spilled out everything-how she thought that Summer might possibly be a reincarnation of Hugh, or that she might be on a same plane with him or that Hugh was communicating with her. Pia told him about all the research that she had done and why she had come to these conclusions. It was a long and difficult speech. When she thought she had made all her points, she sighed and looked up at Craig with sadness on her face.

"Do you think I am an old fool, Craig?"

Craig glanced over at Marla. She was staring into her lap.

"What do you think, Marla?"

She looked up at him timidly.

"I don't know what to think. I listened to all Mom's points. I thought to myself that it was coincidental or genes or environment or any of a number of things. And then Mom showed me the manuscript."

She stopped there suddenly.

"I don't know, Craig. I honestly do not know."

Craig smiled at her.

"You may not believe this, honey, but I was concerned about you. I knew you had something on your mind. You were distracted in a way. Like I said, I was concerned. I wondered if you might be having an affair."

Marla chuckled quietly.

"Oh, if it was only that simple. I didn't know if I should confide in you about this. You are a very understanding man. An open-minded man. And I love you for that. By the way, I would never have an affair. I love you too much and it would be stupid to destroy what we have."

"Then why didn't you confide in me?"

"Because the whole thought is incomprehensible. You are a very pragmatic man. You might think that I, and especially my mother, were taking hallucinogens or something. It is kind of weird, don't you think, Craig?"

Craig put his elbows on the table and buried his face in his hands. He was silent for a few seconds. To Pia and Marla, it seemed like a very long time as they waited for him to speak.

"Yes, it is weird. Nevertheless, I have noticed these inclinations in Summer myself. I have wondered about it. I did not know Hugh for a very long time but I got to know him well and esteemed him. I saw this tendency in Summer to be like him and appreciated it for the fact that a man I esteemed was recurrent in my daughter. As you commented, it could be genes or environment or it could go beyond that. Just because I am pragmatic does not mean that I do not think about or try to understand unearthly ideas or ideas that go beyond the realm."

Pia glanced at him sidelong and spoke softly. "So you do believe in reincarnation?"

"Not necessarily. If you have any thoughts at all, you have to consider an afterlife. You know that I am a religious man and believe in a God. Believing in a God, if you do not believe blindly, takes a lot of thought. Being realistic, I have to ask myself why there are so many religions that all have a supreme deity. Their sacred scriptures tell very much the same chronicles as our Bible. They have the same basic beliefs as we, as Christians, do. Why is so much of the world in accordance with this idea? I said that I am a religious man. I want to change that to spiritual man. The God I happen to worship is the God of Christianity. Does that make a difference? If I was born and raised in India, would I be Hindu? Probably so. Christianity is convenient for me. I do not condemn people who are Buddhist, or Hindu, or Rastafarian. As long as our goals are the same, what does it matter?"

Marla had been sitting back, listening and nodding in agreement. After all, as husband and wife, they had discussed religion and religions many times in the past. It was a mutual part of bonding. An acceptance of their life together. Pia, on the other hand, was sitting forward and listening intently to Craig. She, too, had these same ideas but she wanted to extract more from Craig.

"What are those goals, Craig?"

Craig was a little taken aback that Pia should ask this question. He knew she believed much of what he believed. He wondered if she was baiting him or whether she was going to play the devil's advocate.

"The goals are very simple, Pia. Peace between all men. Do unto your neighbor as you would do unto yourself. The golden rules. Of course, that is very simplified. To follow the golden rules, you must be understanding. You must be tolerant. You must be charitable. You must be loving. You must be forgiving."

Pia stared at him long and hard.

"That is all well and good. All religions have the same goals. Those goals are good. Why don't we all unify into the same spiritual entity? If we all have the same goals and all believe in a single deity- actually it doesn't have to be a single deity- why don't we all merge and become one big happy family? And, for that matter, why are there holy wars?"

Craig thought for a moment.

"They are not holy wars. I don't know why they got that misnomer. Probably because the wars arose between two religions. Like the Catholics and Protestants in Ireland. It is not between Catholicism and Protestantism but between two parties who want control. Actually, it's not between two parties who want control but between several individuals on each side who want control. You know the old question 'What is it you would seek? Would you prefer to have power, money or fame?' I believe that most, if not all wars, are originated because of someone's need and thirst for power. They don't care about money or fame. In fact, they would probably prefer to be anonymous. Yet, they get their way by devious means of propaganda, lies, misdirections, and believability.

"Hitler is a good example. He was a very charismatic person and an excellent speaker. He swayed people easily. I don't know if he really believed that Aryans are supreme but he talked people into believing that. He achieved power <u>and</u> fame. Hitler might have also wanted money because of all the art treasures that were stolen and because of the theft of Jews' money. But I don't think that money was his priority. I think it was, foremost, a feeling of power. He controlled minds!

"There are constant wars ongoing in our world. You never know at one single moment who is fighting whom. It is power seekers who produce these wars. It is also money seekers. They don't care about fame at all. As I said before, they prefer to be anonymous. And best that they stay anonymous. Otherwise, they would be assassinated.

"Who would assassinate them? A religious fanatic? Maybe. Or maybe someone who has learned the truth. John F. Kennedy was assassinated. No one knows why for sure. Perhaps, he knew a truth. His father was powerful and very, very wealthy. He was not completely ethical in his business dealings. Did Kennedy, in his presidency or sometime during his life, discover a secret about international dealings and wars and money moving that his father was involved with? To this day, no one knows for sure why he was assassinated or who really pulled the trigger. Oswald got the heat for it. Was he just a patsy for higher ranks? Ruby killed Oswald. Was he a patsy for higher ranks that were anonymous? Higher ranks that pulled strings and manipulated others like puppets, just as Hitler manipulated people? Higher ranks that wanted money or power?

"In my own opinion, I think the gulf wars have been initiated by powerful persons who want more and more money. Oil! Every country depends on oil. Unknown financiers and bankers manipulate. We have, and many more countries have, the resources to provide our own oil or alternatives to oil. The search for these alternatives has been going on for years. But, somehow, it has become stymied. Why?!!!!! My God! We have sent men into space. We have the ability to clone species. Our computers mimic the human brain. Why don't we have alternative energy? There is alternative energy and lots of it out there. Not to mention that there is enough oil in the bedrock of America to be independent of these other nations. We are puppets of politicians who are puppets of powerful moguls who are unknown. They sit in their offices or chalets or villas and pull the strings. They see themselves as gods. They do reap the money but their real happiness is in power. Power of being a god. We don't know who they are and they like it that way.

"Do we know who our God is? We have pictorials of him as a gentle-looking man, dressed in white and sporting a white beard and long hair. What do you think he looks like, Pia?"

Marla had risen from her chair and disappeared into the kitchen while Craig was speaking. She returned once in a while to pick up the dirty dishes from the table. Pia half rose from her chair to help but Marla motioned for her to stay where she was. She was happy for that. She really wanted to hear more of Craig's opinions. At Craig's last statement, she grimaced.

"Oh dear, Craig! 'What do I think God looks like?' My first thought is what you described. It's etched on our minds since childhood. But you were talking about money managers and power managers and managers of fame. It brought a ridiculous picture to my mind. I thought of Howard Hughes!!!! Near his death, he dressed in white and had a long beard and long hair. He was definitely a man who wanted fame. I don't think he was in the echelons of the people you were mentioning. The *unknowns.* He did achieve fame and maybe he thought of himself as a god. Unfortunately, he went off the deep end. Did his notion of being a god himself make him a lunatic?"

Craig burst out laughing.

"Oh, Pia, you are something else. I see your vision of Howard Hughes and can't control my laughter. You are so right. Maybe old Mr. Hughes did consider himself a god. How many other people consider themselves a god? I think death row might be full of them. Charlie Manson might have been one of them."

Pia leaned back in her chair and put her hands into her lap.

"Yes. And then there are the evangelists. What is their choice? Power, fame, or money?"

"I would say that most of them want the money. There are a few- a very few- that think they are disciples of Christ, but, for the most part, all they're after is money and their fifteen minutes of fame."

"What about power? They claim to heal the sick and perform other miracles. Is that not a claim to power?"

"Yes, it is a claim to power but they are quacks. They trick you into believing that they can perform these miracles. They have power because you believe them and, therefore," Craig rubbed his fingertips together and continued, "they get the money. It's much like the medicine men of the old West. They got up on their soapboxes and proclaimed the magical healing powers of their elixirs. Folks were ailing and couldn't get to or afford a doctor. They bought the elixirs. Most of the elixirs were nothing more than colored water with an additive that made it appear to be medicinal. But, you know what? Some people were actually healed It was not because the elixir cured them but because they *believed* that the elixir had healing powers. It was more of mind over matter than some sham foul-tasting liquid."

Marla had slipped back into her chair.

"Okay, you guys. This is a fascinating debate but aren't you getting off the subject?"

Craig grinned and turned to her.

"Which was?"

"Reincarnation! Do you believe or not?"

"As I said – not necessarily – but I'm open to enlightenment."

Pia intercepted.

"Before we discuss that, I'd like to return to another query I asked."

"Which was?"

"If all religions basically believe in the same thing, why don't they all merge?"

Craig was adamant on this.

"Just as I was saying. The reason there are wars. The reason there are conflicts between peoples of the earth. Because there are people who want fame, power or money. They establish rifts between groups to benefit themselves. They use propaganda. Do you know where the word *propaganda* comes from?" He didn't wait for a reply. "Propaganda is a systematic effort to persuade a body of people to support or adopt a particular opinion. It originates from Congregatio de Propaganda Fide. Also known as the propagation of faith. The council of propagating the faith was instituted by Pope Gregory XV. The council's job was to oversee the foreign missionaries. What beliefs were the council propagating? Were they biased? Were they trying to talk 'dumb ignorant natives' into believing in our Christian god. Many of those 'dumb ignorant natives' had a very strong moral code which they obeyed better than a lot of the missionaries did. Just because they were not Christians did not mean they were sinful people. The natives resented the missionaries coming in to force their beliefs on them. I guess that's why we have the tales of missionaries in boiling pots. There are a great assortment of missionaries. Some are very good. They go to help people improve their means. Albert Schweitzer was a good missionary. He went to Africa to help fight disease there. I don't believe he spread propaganda."

Pia clapped her hands in delight.

" I'm sorry to interrupt but I have an interesting story to tell you about missionaries. It's a true story. It relates what you were talking about, Craig, and it adds to the benevolence that some missionaries can do. Hugh had a friend who he went to school with. Richie eventually became a veterinarian and had a very good and profitable career. I came to know Richie and his wife and the four of us had some good times together. We drank beer together. We traded racy jokes. Jeannine was pretty sexy in a bikini. We talked about a lot of things but I guess we never discussed religion because, all of a sudden, Richie and Jeannine and their two daughters moved to Costa Rica to become missionaries there. It was a total shock to us. In our minds, Richie was definitely not the missionary type. However, he took his family to Costa Rica to help. Not to the wonderful resort area of Costa Rica but up into the mountains where there was nothing but poverty. Richie gave up almost all of his worldly goods to live with his family in a wooden shack in the forests and mountains. His goal was to help the people there with their goats. Goats were the sustenance of the area. They provided milk, meat and wool. Richie was a veterinarian so he taught the Indians how to better care for the goats. The Indians were grateful and loved Richie.

"Richie and Jeannine and the two little girls were very happy and pleased with their new life and felt that God had blessed them. However, there was one more thing that they wanted. They wanted one more child, especially a little boy, to add to their family. Richie and Jeannine tried and tried to conceive but nothing happened. They prayed and prayed and prayed. Then, one day, Jeannine came running to Richie, who was attending to some goats, and announced the good news. She was pregnant! Seven months later, she gave birth to their heart's desire – beautiful baby boy! They were ecstatic. God had blessed them in so many ways. They were fulfilled with their work in the mountains. They had love. They had a beautiful family. They had the friendship and admiration of the Indians. Life was great.

"Then something unbelievable happened! Jeannine was out in her vegetable garden with her two girls, bringing in some crops for dinner. Richie was taking care of goats. The little baby boy was asleep in the cabin. When Jeannine returned to the house with a pail full of corn, she checked on her son. He was not in his bed! He was still an infant. He could not walk yet. Where was he?!!!! She shouted for Richie and he came running. They searched and searched. They ran through the tiny village and questioned every man and woman and child they saw. No one knew anything but they helped the desperate family in their hunt. Days and months went by and no one knew what had happened to the child.

" At this time, San Jose was developing into a big tourist attraction. Huge hotels were being built on the beaches. Guides offered trips into the rain forest to observe the tropical flora and fauna. Much money was coming into the country from turistos. The government did not want the foreigners to see that there was a poverty-stricken area of Costa Rica. They wanted the Indians and the goats out of there. They didn't like Richie being there because he was helping the Indians and encouraging them to stay in their native land and improve themselves. It just didn't look right for this fabulous resort.

"Richie and Jeannine prayed and prayed. One night, Jeannine felt she was dreaming. In her dream, she heard a baby crying. She tossed and turned and then realized the sound was real. She raced out of bed and threw open the front door. There on the wooden porch was a baby in a basket. It was HER baby! It was the little baby boy that she and Richie had prayed for before and after its birth. He was back together with them again! The wonderful news spread through the village like wildfire. Peasants came and went and hugged the grateful parents and brought them gifts of empanadas, black beans with rice, and fried plantains. The whole village was happy and back to normal – Richie helping out with the goats,

Jeannine teaching the women to sew and knit, the girls teaching hopscotch to the Indian girls.

"One evening, during suppertime, there was a knock on the door. Richie opened it, thinking that a goat must be in trouble. It was a humble young man of the village. He knelt down in front of Richie and proffered a knife to him.

"You must kill me, Brother Richie. It was I who took your child. I thought I was doing right. A man from the government came and offered me lots of money to take the baby. He said I could come live down on the beach free for the rest of my life. I would be away from poverty and goats. I could become someone special. I did that, sir. I took the money and I took the baby. I went down to San Juan with my family. The man gave me a place on the beach all right. It was very nice but it led me to the wrong life. I thought I was a man of importance and spent the money unwisely. My wife begged me to take us all back to our home here in the mountains but I was too vain and arrogant. She returned back home but I stayed. Very quickly, the money was gone. I didn't know how to make a living except through goats. I realized my mistakes and I came back to my wife. Now I come to you. I have done a very big sin. You must punish me."

"Richie put his arms under the younger man's arms and lifted him to his feet. He hugged him tenderly. 'Sancho, you have suffered as much as I have. I cannot hurt you but I can help you. It was bad what you did. Yes. But you now know your mistakes and you are repentant. That is all that matters. You are forgiven in my heart. Early tomorrow morning, I want you to come help me with the goats. I will teach you and give you books. Is that a deal?'

"Tears fell from the young man's eyes. 'You are a divine man, Brother Richie. I will do anything for you.' He ran off into the night."

Pia stopped talking. Marla and Craig stared at her. Marla had tears in her eyes.

"Mom, what happened next?"

"I don't know."

"What do you mean – you don't know?"

"All I heard was that particular story. As far as I know, Richie and Jeannine are still living in the mountains of Costa Rica. I think that I did hear that the daughters were sent to England for an education and that they returned to their parents."

"How could Richie afford to send the girls to England if he, too, was living in poverty?"

"I said that Richie gave up MOST of his earthly possessions. He did have a lucrative vet's position. I expect he put away his savings for his daughters."

Craig was scowling.

"GrandPi, did you make up this story?"

"Honestly, I did not. It is the truth as I heard it. Maybe I did embellish on it." She paused for a moment.

"No, I don't think I did embellish on it. My point in telling the story is twofold. Richie was a good missionary. He went to Costa Rica to improve lives because he had skills that he could teach. The temporary loss of the baby is how powerful people try to take control."

Craig was still scowling but nodded at Pia.

"I don't know if I believe your story or not. However it does prove a point. Richie's villager took the baby because he was offered money by powerful people. He thought the money would make his life easier and better. If you're an ignorant man, you listen to what sounds good to you. The things that will make your life probably better and probably easier. We do the same with politicians now. Who do we vote for? We vote for the man or woman who promises a better life. We all know that they are all full of bunk but we vote for them anyway."

Pia wanted more.

"So how do we know what is propaganda and what is truth?"

"Actually, the propaganda could be truth. It is up to us to discover what is the real truth. You know. The truth, the whole truth and nothing but the truth."

It was Marla's turn to interject. "We three are all fairly intelligent people. We try to find out the basic truths. Just as Craig mentioned about investigating all kinds of religions. That's good and gives you a stronger sense of your God. Sometimes, it's hard to find the truth. When an election rolls around, I study the issues. I think about what is best, not just for me but for everyone. I vote for a specific candidate who seems to fulfill what I see as the truth or, at least, partly the truth. Then, I am suddenly disappointed. The candidate's rhetoric was so eloquent that I thought he was expressing the truth. On the other hand, I have sometimes seen beyond the eloquence. I have relied more on sincerity. That seems to work best. However, sincerity- or what appears to be sincerity - does not always work every time either. We are above the average person. I don't mean that in a derogatory way. I just mean that we are well educated. We strive to continue our education in life. We are interested in many facets of life like music, arts, the written word, et cetera. We have the advantage of having the money to indulge in books, go to concerts, eat in fine restaurants, and travel to new places. It constantly expands our minds and lets us open up to new ideas and, perhaps, find the truths.

" Now, what about the average Joe? I'm using the term average as a medium. There are the super rich, the upper middle class, the middle class, the lower middle class and the poor. In our economy, it would seem to me that the demographics would show that there are more people in the United States who fall into the lower class and poor category than into the other categories. This is just an assumption on my part but I will continue on with point. The lower class and the poor usually have not had the opportunity of a good education either by schooling or by experience. It seems to me that they would be easily affected by fancy rhetoric or propaganda It would be hard for them to distinguish *real* truths."

Craig was admiring his wife.

"You are right, Marla. Unforunately, that's where the evangelists and many wholesale preachers make their money. They promise the kingdom of heaven to these suckers. The notion of a better life and the kingdom of heaven is ingrained in their heads but only if they contribute to the coffers. The pork barrel politicians prey upon them in the same way. "

Marla looked sad. "Isn't there a way we can improve this situation?"

Pia spoke up. "I liked the idea of the Peace Corps. The Peace Corps volunteers helped the less advantaged to improve their lives. How to farm better. How to raise livestock more successfully. That is what they are best known for. And there are groups that go to inner cities and provide books and other educational tools to aide in better development of the mind. As far as I know, they didn't propagandize anything harmful. Whether people took advantage of this help was up to them. Some people want to improve but some people just want to lay back and let the rest of the world take care of them. They become dependent on welfare because it's an easy way out. Sometimes, it's hard to dig yourself out of a bad situation. Studying takes a lot of concentration and effort. Some people don't want the effort. They are lazy. Or they turn to drugs. And that takes us back to the nabobs. The unknown power seekers. They have nothing to do with drugs themselves but they control a drug trade."

Craig beamed.

"And here we are back to that same conversation! I agree with your reference to the Peace Corps. There are a lot of groups out there that are not as well recognized but are instrumental in helping the disadvantaged to realize their potential."

Pia sat upright.

"That's it. That's a word that I wanted to get to this evening. Potential! Potential is a very powerful word. Noetics believe that if everyone channels their inner consciousness with others, new and wonderful works can be initiated. Wait a minute. I'm putting this poorly. It's more like if everyone channels their ideas and potential with others, the world expands and understands new and original concepts."

She giggled a little.

"Do you remember the coneheads on Saturday Night Live? That's how I envision this idea. A bunch of coneheads all touch the tips of their cones together. It's like a tepee and, all of a sudden, a laser beam flies out from the top of the tepee and a new concept or idea is originated."

Marla and Craig laughed but loved the image.

"Mom, did you bring over your cone this evening? Maybe we can make some out of construction paper, put our heads together and solve the world's problems."

"Don't laugh at me. I just might grow one of my own cones and get together with some other coneheads and we'll become rich and famous and powerful. No, forget I said that. What I wanted to express is another idea that's out there."

Craig was getting silly as he patted her hand.

"Where is 'there', GrandPi?"

"Don't make fun of me. There is there."

She swept her arm around to envelop everything surrounding her.

"I am going back to potential again. There is a concept *out there* that believes you can develop your own potential. Of course we all know that and strive for that. Look at those masters of karate who can chop a cement block in half with the side of their hand. They do it by using their mind and potential. Yoga is a great form of potential. But *these* advocates say that as you continually develop your potential, you become more and more improved in every way."

Marla yawned.

"There is no argument in that."

"I know but it goes beyond that. *These* people believe that we all have the potential to be Gods. That God is present within all of us. That as we improve our minds, we become more and more Godlike and eventually are a God."

Marla yawned again.

"There is a quote form the bible that says 'God is within you."

"Yes, I know that but *these* people say that the God within you is a potential to become God."

Pia noticed Marla yawn again and glanced at her watch. Oh my God! It was one o'clock already. No wonder Marla was yawning. She wasn't bored. She was tired. She giggled inwardly to herself. She shouldn't have thought 'oh, my God'. She should have thought 'for Pete's sake.'

"I'm sorry, my dears. I didn't realize how late it was. I must be going and let you all go to bed. And we still haven't gotten around to reincarnation."

Craig stood up.

"Wait just a minute, GrandPi. I have something to show you. It will give you something to think about when you drift asleep tonight."

He ran off toward his office. Pia looked curiously at Marla who shrugged her shoulders in return. *I dunno.*

Craig returned shortly with a piece of paper in his hand. He smiled bemusingly as he handed the paper to Pia.

"Read this. You asked me about reincarnation. I don't know. I came upon this not too long ago and I have thought about it. What a coincidence that our conversation tonight pointed to this poem. It was written by an Islamic poet named Jalal al-Din Muhammad Rumi."

Pia took the slip of paper from Craig's hand and read it.

"I died as inanimate matter and arose a plant,
I died as a plant and rose again an animal.
I died as an animal and arose a man.
Why then should I fear to become less by dying?
I shall die once again as a man
To rise an angel perfect from head to foot!
Again when I suffer dissolution as an angel,
I shall become what passes the conception of man!
Let me then become non-existent, for non-existence

Sings to me in organ tones, 'To Him shall we return.'"

Pia gasped. She turned to Craig and barely muttered. "So does this mean you believe?"

"I don't know, GrandPi. It's a lot to think about. I read this and thought it interesting and then I listened to your thoughts tonight. It certainly is food for the brain."

"That it is, Craig, and I will go to bed thinking, thinking, thinking. Hopefully, I will fall asleep."

She reached out to Marla and hugged her. She started to walk out the door and then came back to hug Craig too.

"It has been an interesting evening."

"That it has been. And I will let you leave with another quote from Pope. 'Conversation is the feast of reason and the flow of soul.'"

"Aha, the idea of soul is another good conversation."

With that closing remark, Pia disappeared into the night.

21.

I t was early spring. Summer had been working for the *New Yorker* and was furiously engaged in writing another book. She had been off to lectures and book signings. Pia had not seen her for a long time and missed her. It seemed that everyone's life had taken a different direction since Sweden.

A beautiful sun-filled day awakened Pia. The temperature was moderate. In the mid-sixties. She threw on some sweats and had her coffee on the deck. Surveying her yard, she thought about what she wanted to do- what she wanted to do for the planting of the yard and what she wanted to do for the rest of the year. After dumping her toast plate and coffee cup in the dishwasher, she grabbed her gardening gloves and gardening utensils. Replanting the dahlia and canna lily bulbs that had pulled in the fall, she heard a car door slam. Not expecting any company, Pia continued to dig in the fresh spring dirt. It was not long before she heard footsteps quietly traipsing across her back lawn. She rubbed her garden gloves across her forehead, leaving a streak of mud. Someone tapped her on the shoulder and she turned around. It was Summer. Pia rose from her kneeling position to give Summer a big hug.

"No, don't touch me, GrandPi. You are all muddy!"

Summer laughed.

"Well, let's go up to the house and I'll clean up. Then will you hug me?"

"Of course. I'll even hug you now. I don't mind getting dirty. I was just kidding."

"Just wait a moment. I just have these three more bulbs to plant. Then I'll be through and we can sit on the deck and chat. It's a gorgeous day, isn't it?"

Pia knelt back down on the soft earth and resumed her chores.

"Yes, GrandPi, it is. And you know what?"

"What?"

"I think you are beautiful with mud on your face."

"Okay, I've had enough of your bullshit. I'm through. Help me up."

Summer took Pia's arm and pulled her up . They walked arm in arm up the steps to Pia's deck. Pia kicked off her clogs.

"Sit down, Summer, while I clean up. Have you had lunch yet?"

"No, I haven't but don't fix something just for me."

"The hell with you. I'm hungry and you might as well share with me. "

Summer loved her grandmother. She had so much spunk! She laughed.

"Okay, GrandPi. I want chateaubriand with a demi-glaze, caramelized new potatoes, and asparagus with hollandaise."

"Coming up. Just give me a couple of minutes."

Pia disappeared into the house and Summer settled herself into one of the wicker chairs. She looked around. It was a nice little place that her grandmother kept. It was still early spring but she could visualize what it would look like in another month. The weeping willow by the pond was already starting to green up. Flowers that GrandPi had planted would be sprouting all over in various gardens. By mid-summer, the entire back yard would be a spectacle of blues, and reds and, yellows, and greens, and purples. Not to mention the birds. The hummingbirds that came to the butterfly bush and assorted flowers. The bright yellow finches that frequented the finch feeder. Of course, the butterflies frequented the butterfly bush, too. It would not be too long before the fireflies would be appearing in the evening. She smiled and thought about the times when she and

Eric had come over on summer nights. GrandPi would hand each of them a Mason jar and give them a nickel for each firefly they caught. At the end of the evening, all the fireflies would be released. Summer wanted to keep just one to keep in a jar in her room at home.

No, darling. Fireflies belong in the sky. Not in a jar in your room.

Who had told her that? It wasn't GrandPi. It had been a man's voice. She could still hear it. She wondered who it had been. Probably some friend of Grandpi.

Summer was totally relaxed. The deck was primarily decorated in shades of yellow. The chairs and table were yellow. Interesting. In Vedic mythology, yellow is the color of spring and activates the mind. That is so true, she thought. GrandPi was the most active in the springtime. Planting bulbs and flowers. Cleaning up the yard. Redoing the deck. Yellow suited her. And yellow is the color of knowledge and learning. It symbolizes happiness, peace, meditation, competence, and mental development. What a wonderful and predictable color for GrandPi to choose. But, then, there were the accent blues. Blue for-get-me-nots intertwined on the yellow seat cushions. A blue tablecloth focusing the yellow candle in the center of the table. The Vedic deity who has the qualities of bravery, manliness, determination, the ability to deal with difficult situations, of stable mind and depth of character is represented as blue-colored. The sky, oceans, lakes and rivers are blue. GrandPi always likes to have water near her. Summer wondered if the color scheme had been selected when her grandfather was still alive. From what she knew of him, he matched Pia very well. She had slumped down in her chair to ponder, splaying her long legs in front of her. She could hear bees buzzing and birds chirping and then the sound of the patio door thumping. She jumped out of her chair.

"Good God, GrandPi! Why didn't you ask me to help you?"

Pia was struggling out the door with a huge tray.

"I don't need help. I can handle it."

Summer held the door as Pia moved through and set the tray on the table. She arranged place settings for both of them.

"Summer, this may not look like chateaubriand to you, but, believe me, it is. I just have my own special recipes. My chateaubriand looks like chicken salad. My caramelized new potatoes look like croissants with a honey butter finish and my asparagus looks like fresh grapes Oh, and my fine wine looks like lemonade."

"It looks grand to me."

Summer spread her napkin on her lap and stared at her grandmother. She had so many questions to ask her. One was the reason for the yellow plates and blue stemware. That was incidental. She also suspected that her grandmother had a lot of questions to ask her.

Pia took a bite of chicken salad and a bite of her croissant. She washed it down with a big sip of lemonade and then confronted Summer.

"Okay, Summer. What brings you here today? I know that you are working hard at your job. I know that you are traveling a lot. I know that you are working on another book. What made you come by to have lunch with me?"

Summer put down her fork and leaned back in her chair. She put her palms together as if in prayer and raised them next to her nose and mouth. She stared at Pia for a moment. Pia pretended that she did not notice and continued to eat.

"GrandPi."

"Yes?"

Pia looked up as if startled.

"GrandPi, what do you think about me?"

"Oh my God, child. I love you."

"I know that but you know something else about me."

It was Pia's turn to put her fork down. She frowned and squinted at Summer. "And what is that supposed to mean?"

Summer ran her fingers through her hair and contemplated for a moment. She was trying to phrase this correctly.

"Mom asked me something the other day."

"And what was that?"

"She asked me if I had ever seen the files that you have of my grandfather's works."

This time, Pia leaned back in her chair. She was mad at her daughter for bringing this up. Marla had no right. It was done. It

145

didn't need to be brought up again. Summer had won the Nobel Prize. It didn't matter where her notes had come from. Of course, reincarnation was a different matter and Pia wondered if Marla had brought up that subject, too. She was trying to be cool. Very cool. However, she did fold her arms in defiance. And, this time, it was in defiance.

"So what did you tell her?"

"I didn't know that you had any notes on grandfather's future books."

"Is that the honest truth?"

Summer leaned her elbows on the table, put her hands up to her face and gazed at Pia.

"GrandPi, what is this all about? I can see that you are obviously upset about something."

Pia thought about what to say. She didn't know exactly what Marla had told Summer. She sat up again in her chair.

"Summer, I didn't ever want your mother to mention this to you. I am not accusing you of stealing your grandfather's notes. Did she mention what the notes were?"

"No."

Pia relaxed a little, but put her elbows on the table, her head down in contemplation and ran her fingers through her hair. What could she say to Summer next? Summer was staring at her. She knew it. She had to say something. Anything.

"Summer, when exactly did you get the ideas for your Nobel -winning book."

"Oh, I don't know. I think I told you long ago that after I learned the truth about Santa and the Easter bunny, I questioned a lot of things. I still went to church with Mom and Dad but I questioned it. Was Jesus just another made-up person to make us feel good? I mean, this is still when I was in elementary school. I never said anything to Mom or Dad or anyone else for that matter. It was just a question in my mind. And then when you learn World History in school, there are so many myths and legends that are concerned. Do you really think that Romulus and Remus really founded Rome after being suckled by a wolf? Of course not. But some peoples had believed that. Well, going back again to elementary school. You read the stories about Pecos Bill and Paul Bunyan and Johnny Appleseed. We really didn't believe that Pecos Bill dug the Rio Grande River but why was that story made up?"

"It's called fakelore, Summer. I'm sure that there was a cowboy out there who was incredibly good at what he did. And a lumberjack who was terrific at what he did. And there really was a Johnny Appleseed."

"I know all of that, GrandPi. But why do people have to make up these stories and exaggerations? Of course, that is why I wrote the book. But, to answer your question, I guess it all started in grade school."

"Did it make you a pessimist? I never saw you as a pessimist or cynic."

"No, incredibly, it didn't. It did make me look at people differently."

"How so?"

Summer leaned back in her chair and thought for a while. It seemed to Pia that she was thinking for a long time. Then Summer finally responded.

"GrandPi. Every spring, you come out here and plant and weed and plant and hoe and water and mulch. You believe that by the late spring and all through summer, you will have beautiful flowers growing."

"It's not a belief, Summer, it's a fact. That's why I mulch and weed and water – to ensure that my flowers will come up beautifully."

"Okay. That's correct. But….."

"But what?"

"How many times have I driven down a highway with you and listened to you remark on the beautiful flowers or bushes or trees growing up wild along the side of the road. Nobody nurtures them."

"But they are put there haphazardly. I plan my gardens so they are not haphazard."

"Exactly. Just as people plan their lives. They need a structure to it. They don't want things to happen haphazardly. They create stories like Pecos Bill because it made more sense than a glacier or earth upheaval to form a river. They made up religions to explain how the world came about."

Pia frowned.

"How do you explain the many religions? And how they are all related. Every religion has it's holy book. Each holy book has stories that are somewhat the same. For example, most of them have a story of a great flood."

Summer grinned.

"Yes, and there is evidence of a great flood of the Earth. But was there a Noah? A Noah who saved his family and all the species of the animals? That is a fairy tale. Besides, it's contradictory. As religious students, we are taught that we are all the products of Adam and Eve. But! If no one but Noah and his family and all the animals were saved then we are all the descendants of Noah."

Pia laughed.

"And then where do we classify Darwin?"

"GrandPi, I think you are trying to trap me. You know I believe in Darwin's theory on the evolution of the species."

"Yes you do and so do I. Now, what do you think of theosophy?"

"In regards to what?"

Pia knew she was entering a new concept and had to walk on eggshells here.

"That theosopists believe in reincarnation. Many people think about reincarnation. But most of them think about what animal they'd like to come back as or something like that. Theosophists believe that the reincarnated person comes back with a - how can I put it? – a regenerated brain. A superior brain, so that the human race continues to improve. It's like Darwin's theory of the evolution of the species. People die, come back and are better and/or smarter people than before. What do you think about that?"

"GrandPi, you are baiting me again. I have thought that reincarnation is another way of people's way of dealing with life after death. They don't want to think that, once you die, you are just reduced to ashes. That's how heaven and hell were created.

And that's where reincarnation comes into the picture. Is there a heaven where everything is ideal? Is there a hell where you are tortured forever? Another option is reincarnation. If you're not going to get into heaven, hopefully you'll get a second chance by being reincarnated. But the theosophist's theory is very interesting in regards to Darwin."

Summer put her fingertips together. Pia thought to herself – *here is the church, here is the steeple* – but she didn't want to interrupt Summer and tried to keep a straight face.

Summer continued on.

"The world is definitely evolving. I don't know how what we call the animal kingdom is evolving. I am not a zoologist and don't have any particular interest in that field except for having a dog as a pet. But homo sapiens is evolving. People are taller than they were a couple hundred years ago. That's a type of evolution. My main concern in having this discussion with you is whether humans are evolving intellectually. It's hard to say. We look around us and see what has been invented in the past three hundred years. That's just a miniscule drop in the history of mankind. Electricity was invented. No, discovered. As a result of electricity, all kinds of things were invented. We are now in the computer age because man has discovered how to emulate the brain. Isn't that quite a bit of progress in just a relatively short amount of time? But then you think about DaVinci and his contributions to the world of art and, particularly, science. He lived during the fifteenth century. Look at all the art that came out of the renaissance period. As a matter of fact, art came about very early in the development of mankind. Primitive man was creating quite good art. But to go back to DaVinci. If he was reincarnated, who did he and his brain become. Albert Einstein?!!!! And how long does it take for a person to be reincarnated to another person? Does it happen right away or does it take a couple hundred years?

"And that brings me to another subject. Noetic Science. Have you heard of it, GrandPi?"

Pia tried to act serene while the back of her head remembered the very vivid dream.

"I've heard of it but don't know a whole lot about it."

"Well, it's basically a science that believes that the human mind has a lot more potential than it uses. If all the potential is used, then it could be channeled."

Pia had to stifle a chuckle as she thought about her reference to the coneheads. She pretended to play dumb and looked at her granddaughter curiously.

"Channeled?"

"Yes, channeled. Great minds can work together to submerge into one propelling force and accomplish anything like using kinetic force or controlling nature . "

"Do you believe this?"

"I'm not sure. It is very interesting and somewhat credible. However, my point in bringing this up is that the people who believe in noetic science also believe that the ancients had the wisdom of this. The ancients held the secrets to powers of the mind and were reluctant to reveal them. Now, that might be another myth. I came across this in my research for my Nobel book. But, if there is reincarnation? Could someone from a time before Christ have knowledge of having extraordinary mental power? Then he dies. He is reincarnated into da Vinci. Da Vinci dies. He is reincarnated as Einstein. Einstein dies. Who has been reincarnated from him?"

Summer had sat up part way through delivering this discourse. Pia tried to read her body language. To her, it seemed that Summer was rethinking a few things. Then Summer looked at her full in the face. It was *the look.* Pia still didn't understand the look. It still appeared that Summer was trying to look into her soul. Was she trying to communicate something that she couldn't express verbally? But Summer continued to talk and Pia didn't want to interrupt her thoughts. She had thoughts of her own. *Summer, was your grandfather reincarnated a couple of years after he died?*

"But I don't know if I believe in that reincarnation spiel." Summer continued. " I believe it's just another myth and you know I've done enough research on that. Couldn't it just be a case of genetics? The parents have good intelligent genes and pass them on to their offspring. That's a very good explanation and makes the most sense to me. Plus, it's the environment. Obviously, if you are bred in an environment that encourages education and learning and perfecting yourself, you are going to progress. That makes more sense than reincarnation.

"By the way, GrandPi, what's for dessert?"

"Oh, my dear, I completely forgot. I'll be right back."

"GrandPi, I was just kidding. I don't need any dessert."

"Yes, you do. You're as skinny as a rail. I'll be right back and I think I have something you'll like."

Pia rushed into the kitchen. She needed to get away from Summer for a while and reorganize her thoughts. Apparently Marla had not mentioned reincarnation to her. She simply asked Summer about the notes and if she had seen them. Why had Summer brought up noetics? It all seemed so coincidental. Her dream and then her discussion with Marla and Craig.

It's coincidental. It's like planning to have chicken for dinner, but you don't know how to fix it. You have spinach and yams in the refrigerator. Later on, you turn on the food network, and there is someone fixing a fantastic dish with spinach and yams. Coincidental? Happenstance? Or it's like when you decide to do something new with your hair. You have a pretty good idea of what you want in your mind. As soon as you sit down in the salon chair, the stylist says "I know what would look really good on you" and proceeds to fix your hair just as you had envisioned. The next day, you have lunch with a friend. She admires your new 'do' and says "You know what? It's funny but I saw that cut in a magazine the other day and thought how great it would look on you."

Accidental? Circumstantial? Is that what this is all about with Summer and my thoughts about Summer?

Summer's thoughts about reincarnation were very good but that still did not explain a few things to Pia. Why had Summer picked a particular subject for her book if she had no idea about the notes? How had she recognized Stan Morrow at her tenth birthday party and then picked him to be her agent? And *the look.* Pia had another scary thought. Maybe Summer was not a reincarnation of her grandfather. Maybe Hugh was trying to communicate with her using Summer as a medium. She had to sit down for a minute and think this idea over. Why had she not thought of this before? Her hands and legs were shaking.

In the meantime, Summer rose from her chair and walked to the deck railing to gaze at GrandPi's yard. No doubt, she had a green thumb. It was still early spring but already the formation of what the yard would look like in another month was taking shape. The lilacs had buds on them. There were sprouts coming up where daffodils and tulips would appear. The crocuses were already displaying their purple, white and yellow cloaks. The sun had gotten warmer and the frogs were croaking in the pond.

She wondered what was taking GrandPi so long. Surely she was not baking a dessert especially for her! She wandered over to the sliding door and called in. "GrandPi?! Everything okay?"

"Sure, honey, I just went in to put a sweater on. It's not quite as warm out when I'm not working. I'll be right out with a surprise for you."

Pia ran into the bedroom to grab a light jacket so she could prove her point and not have to explain her absence to Summer. She took a deep breath, grabbed up the dessert plates and went back to the deck.

"Oh my, GrandPi! Key lime pie! You know it's my favorite. Did you know I was coming over?"

"No, but I made two of them and was planning to bring one over for you."

"Now you don't have to. I just might eat the whole intended pie right now."

Pia watched her granddaughter plunge into the pie. Strange. That was Hugh's favorite dessert, too. That's not communication with the dead. That's coincidence – *or something.*

"I've been looking at your gardens, GrandPi. They are going to be as lovely as ever."

"I'm glad you think so. Let's get back to my gardens for a minute. I plant seeds. It's miraculous that a tiny seed, just a few centimeters in diameter, can produce these huge and astonishing flowers or vegetables or herbs. Not to mention human reproduction. A tiny sperm travels up a canal and finds an ovum. Smack!"

Pia smacked the tips of her two index fingers together to demonstrate her point.

"Yes, and isn't that haphazard? Even your flowers are somewhat haphazard. They also reproduce and bear fruit themselves through pollination. Who knows what bee or butterfly will go to which flower or bush?"

"I'll concede that to you. However, what was I doing when you stopped by?"

"Planting bulbs. Why?"

"In the fall, I dig up the bulbs of dahlias and cannas and some others. I put them in a garbage can filled with shredded paper. They stay there all winter undisturbed until I plant them again like I was just doing. Other bulbs like daffodils or tulips stay in the ground all winter because they can take the winter freeze. But they have long since stopped blooming. For all practical purposes, they are dead. The leaves and stems withered and dried and died long ago. But….. by springtime, they come to life again. They are rejuvenated. They are reincarnated!"

"But, GrandPi, you are talking about plants not living creatures."

"In my opinion, plants are living creatures. Haven't you ever heard the theory that plants might cry 'ouch' when you pull them up or that they are healthier when you talk to them? But I digress. Listen, what do you hear?"

"I just heard a car going down the street. I hear some children's voices in the distance. I hear your wind chimes."

"Do you hear anything else?"

"I hear the sound of our voices and the clink of our forks on the plates."

"And what else? It's something you would not have heard a month ago."

"Okay, yes. I hear the frogs."

"Yes. You didn't hear them a month ago because they were dormant. They hibernate. They bury themselves in the mud and all vital signs are shut down for a partial amount of time. Couldn't that happen to humans? We say they die. The vital signs are shut down. And, then, boom! The vital signs are resurrected. Of course, the body has rotted by then and has no earthly importance except to fertilize the ground."

"GrandPi, look what you are saying. The body rots. That means the brain rots. The heart rots. How could someone be reincarnated?"

"The soul, Summer, the soul! That doesn't rot. I'm sure that with all your studies, you've done enough about the existence of a soul."

Summer pushed her plate aside, stood up again and looked to the sky. There was nothing there but a few cirrus clouds and a very beautiful blue background.

"Look at what I'm looking at."

Pia looked up into the sky.

"I see clouds and sky. Oh, wait a minute, I think I see a jet stream and maybe there's a bird or a plane way off there."

"Don't get smartass on me. Do you see angels hovering around? Do you see weeping souls or joyful souls? After all, isn't that where they are supposed to be? Up in the great firmament?"

Pia lowered her head and whispered, "Souls are invisible."

"Pardon me?"

Pia picked up her head.

"Souls are invisible!" She said this much louder than she intended to. It was almost a scream.

Summer leaned toward her.

"GrandPi. What are you trying to tell me? I have a feeling that you are making it a point. Is it that you believe in reincarnation? I mean, that's okay with me if that's what you want to believe. I don't have a problem with Mom and Dad practicing their religion. I don't have a problem with you believing in reincarnation. Just because I don't believe in these things doesn't mean that I don't love all of you and respect you for your beliefs. I am open- minded enough to let other people have their beliefs. I just happen to not believe in those things myself."

"Summer, do you believe in love?"

"Well, hell, I guess I do. I certainly love you and Mom and Dad and my siblings and cousins, et cetera, et cetera. I've never loved a man the way that you apparently loved my grandfather. I know my parents have a strong love for each other. I've seen this in other couples. I've never felt that type of love."

"Summer, what is love about? Is it part of the brain or part of the soul?"

Summer stood up and started pacing the deck. Her arms were folded and there was a determined look on her face. Pia watched her go back and forth and back and forth in silence. Summer stopped her pacing and leaned against the railing, facing Pia.

"It's the brain. You love someone because you trust in them, you rely on them . I love the people I love because they are good to me and satisfy my needs."

"Is that all you feel about me? I fill your needs? I'm insulted, Summer. I thought I meant more to you than that. I think it's time you go home."

Pia knew she was taking a chance but she wanted to challenge Summer's thoughts.

Summer had turned around and was now looking at the pond. Pia could hardly hear her next words.

"GrandPi, I think I will go home. I have some thinking to do. You've confused me. Plus, I've got to get some work done. I've got an article due in a couple of days."

She turned around and rushed toward Pia. It was a very quick hug but Pia could feel the tears on Summer's cheeks.

Pia pulled her back but held onto her shoulders.

"My dear Summer, you said something to me on the way back from Sweden. You said 'I want to believe in a God. It helps the soul.' What are your thoughts on that now?"

Tears were swelling heavily in Summer's eyes now. She turned and ran to her car.

22.

The phone rang at precisely eleven o'clock the next morning. Pia was pretty sure who it was. She had been looking in the refrigerator to see what to have for lunch after she put in another hour in her gardens.

"Good morning, Summer."

"How'd you know it was me?"

"Just had a feeling. What's up?"

"Wanna go out to lunch? My treat."

"I'd love to go out to lunch with you, my dear. And it is your treat because it was my treat yesterday."

"Fair enough. Where do you wanna go? Ruby Tuesday's? I feel like a good salad."

Pia couldn't resist and felt like she should be wearing a Groucho Marx disguise, raising her eyebrows and waving a cigar.

"Well, I'm sure you don't look like a salad."

"Ha ha, GrandPi. Is Ruby Tuesday's okay with you?"

"Fine but I don't think it really matters. It sounds like you've made up your mind already."

"Sorry, didn't mean to do that. Is there someplace else you'd like to go?"

"No, that's fine. What time?"

Summer was already sitting in a booth and nursing a scotch and water when Pia arrived. The server showed up almost immediately and took Pia's order for a glass of Pinot Grigio and salads for both of them.

"Well, wanna go get some salad, Summer?"

"Not just yet. I want to talk first. I was rude to you yesterday."

"No you weren't. You were just expressing your opinions."

"I've been doing a lot of thinking about the soul and love."

"I knew you would. That's how I knew it was you when you called this morning."

Summer smiled and leaned back into the banquette.

"I know. That's why I always come to you. You don't ever equivocate with me."

"But you don't tell me everything. You hold back on a lot of stuff. Not just to me but to other people too."

Summer took another sip of her scotch and whirled the liquid around in the glass while she considered her response.

"You're right and it's not because I am trying to hide anything. I'm trying to figure it out in my own mind first. I want to go back to yesterday's conversation."

"Okay."

"We were talking about love and the existence of a soul."

"That's correct."

"Let me go off on another tangent for a moment. When did you fall in love with my grandfather?'

Pia was somewhat taken aback by this line of questioning but it was easy to answer the question. She took a deep breath.

"Well, Summer, I liked him—had a great attraction to him- from the moment we first met. There was not a moment when I suddenly realized that I loved him. The feelings grew and intensified. Perhaps, I did say to myself one day, 'I love this man.' But I don't remember a particular day or time or moment. You know? I can go back to the analogy of my plants. I watch them sprout out of the ground. A little green shoot sticking up from the earth. Then it grows higher and maybe develops some leaves. A bud appears. Just a simple little bud but you know what is going to happen. The next thing you know is there is a flower. A beautiful flower. Bright colored petals open to the sun. Raising it's arms to the sky and exulting in its beauty. That's the best way I can describe how love developed for me."

Summer frowned and looked into her empty glass and pondered. She had not been thinking about having another drink but the server reappeared and asked if they would both like refills. They both nodded yes. He also reminded them that the salad bar was there for them to enjoy any time they wanted. Pia and Summer grinned at each other.

"Do you think the server would like us to get some salad, eat it up, and leave so he has another booth free?"

"I don't know but we better get something to eat if we are going to have another drink."

Summer was trying to position a piece of olive, lettuce, pepper, and cheese on her fork. Her brow was furrowed in concentration. Pia was not sure if it was the salad or Summer's next question that was taking up her attention. Summer solved it for her. She put down her fork.

"GrandPi. I know a couple people who have mental illnesses. They take drugs to put their minds in order. The mental illness is a kind of brain disorder. The drug puts them into a kind of normality. Who knows what normality is, but that is beside the fact. Do you think that if a doctor gave you a drug to alter your mind that it would have changed your feelings for my grandfather? Now, I am not saying you were crazy to 'fall in love' with my grandfather." Summer emphasized her use of 'fall in love' by making quotation marks in the air.

"I am just curious to see if it is chemicals in the brain that make people love each other."

"Summer, you are too smart for your own good. You overanalyze too much. There are so many kinds of love. I know you love your parents. I know you love me. That is one kind of love. You expressed yesterday that love is a trust and/or dependency on another person."

Summer started to protest but Pia held her finger up to her lips to shush her.

"It is true that as babies, and even into our teens, we love our parents for what they do for us. Then, when we mature, we realize what our parents have done for us and we love them even more. And then, we realize that we love them for who they are and not for what they've done for us. We love them for who they are. Actually, we have loved them for who they are since we were little children but we don't come to the realization of that fact until we are older.

"And then there are siblings, and other relatives and friends. Some we accept more than others. Okay, we love some more than others. Our friends are a difficult theory to explain in your terms of thought. We are attracted to certain people. They may have interests in common with you. Usually, that's the case. But I have a couple of friends who I have nothing in common with. Our politics don't agree. We practice different religions. We don't like the same type of music or the same type of food. If you get down to it, we probably disagree on a lot of things. ***But*** there's an aura about them to which I am attracted.

"And that's the way about all kinds of love – between families, between friends and , especially, between life mates. This aura is what I call *soul*. Soul is not a chemical. Soul is unexplainable. Soul is what makes you choose your friends. It makes you choose between country music and zydeco. It makes you prefer chicken and dumplings over coq au vin. It makes you prefer the color blue rather than the color green. And soul is what makes you chose your lover."

Summer laughed.

"GrandPi, it's interesting that you said lover. Isn't lover a person you lust over? And isn't that chemicals?"

Pia smiled at her over the rim of her wine glass.

"My dear, you are very smart and wise in many ways, but there are ways you are not too wise in. I worry about you. You know so much for your age but you also know so little. A lover does not necessarily have to be someone you lust for. A lover is someone whom you are attracted to by some kind of magnetism."

"Ah, yes! And where does that magnetism come from? Chemicals in the brain, perhaps? In fact, there have been studies to that effect.

There are certain chemicals between two people that make them attract each other."

Pia felt like she was losing the battle. She ate her salad in silence for a few minutes. If Summer was a reincarnation of Hugh or if Hugh was using Summer as a medium, was the love between them just the result of chemicals? All of a sudden she felt very depressed. She poked at her salad. *No! The love between me and Hugh was too strong! It was not chemicals!*

"Summer, I'm not going to get into a discussion of God with you because I want to be more basic. I'm going back to soul. There are so many things that happen in this world that are inexplicable even to scientists. Look at birth. It's been happening since the beginning. Yes, we know that a male produces sperm to fertilize a woman's eggs. That's a general plan in the animal kingdom. Now, I want to know one thing. Why on Earth did Adam think of plunging his penis into Eve's vagina? Is that a natural thing to do? But it goes farther back. If we are evolved from monkeys and the monkeys evolved from some other species and so on, why did they think of copulating?"

"Because they are animals, GrandPi. Animals do all sorts of strange things. If we are evolved from monkeys, the mind-set to copulate was in the brain for the human."

"But it seems to me that the animals know what they are doing. They copulate to produce children. There is that mating instinct in them."

"GrandPi, just as you said – that is an instinct, not soul."

"Aha! That's what I thought you'd say. After a child is born, there is a maternal instinct. The mother nurtures and protects. In some classes of animals, the father nurtures and protects. But no species of animals leaves their young to fend for themselves."

Pia stopped for a minute and thought.

"Except maybe turtles!"

Summer laughed.

"And you're saying that parental instinct is soul."

"Exactly, my dear."

"I'll have to work on that."

"Summer, let me tell you a little story. I do believe that parental instinct is soul. But that instinct can carry on to other things. Last year, there was a vine growing near the edge of my deck. You know that I have planned plantings. It's somewhat like planned parenthood. Anyway, I let that vine grow and watched it and watched it. I was pretty sure I knew what it was and I wasn't going to disturb it. Sure enough, it turned out to be a watermelon vine and produced a wonderful juicy watermelon. Just as I thought that my children and grandchildren were the best ever produced, so was that watermelon. It had a dark green rind and the most beautiful pink flesh. And, boy, was it yummy. The only way I can think of it growing there was that someone had spit watermelon seeds over my deck and this vine developed. Wasn't that wonderful! An ugly little black seed that someone had spit out had developed into a gorgeous and delicious fruit. I had nurtured it and protected it. It was the soul within me. Just as the soul within me nurtures and protects everything else I grow. And most importantly, my own children and grandchildren. There! I've tried to deliver my point."

"And a good point you've made. I'm going to have to deliberate on this. I must get going now to deliberate."

"You do that, dear. And I've got to be going, too. I've got a dinner date with Jason."

"Who's Jason?"

"An old friend. We get together occasionally and have dinner and bullshit."

"Well, don't get any animal instincts going on between you two."

Pia looked at her with false sternness.

"I don't think you should be telling me how to conduct my life. I'll do whatever I want to do. I've earned that right at my stage of my life."

Summer coyly twirled her hair around a finger.

"GrandPi, you've earned that right at any stage of your life. But I have to tell you something."

Pia sat up in the booth.

"And what's that?"

"I've got a date tonight, too."

"Anyone I know?"

"I don't think so. But this is our third date."

Pia raised her eyebrows.

"He doesn't mind you rushing home to work on your investigations?"

"Actually, he has helped me. I can bounce ideas off him."

"Sounds like this is more than your third date."

"No, this actually is our third date but we do communicate over the phone and e-mail."

"So, how do you feel about this man?"

"I don't know. He is very interesting. I can suggest ideas to him and he responds. It's like he's more interested in my mind than my body."

"First of all, Summer, is he using you? What does he do for a living?"

"He's a math professor. I don't think what I do reflects in any way on what he does."

"Good, good."

Then Pia had to smirk.

"Are you saying that your other dates have been using you for your body? You do have a good one, you know."

"GrandPi, I'm in my late twenties. Don't you think that I have primal instincts, too?"

"Summer, you shock me!"

Pia laughed.

"Come on. We gotta get out here and primp for our dates."

"But I don't have to primp, GrandPi. Jim accepts me as I am."

Summer took care of the check and, by mutual agreement, Pia left the gratuity. They slid out of the booth, and went in their separate directions.

On the drive home, Pia smiled to herself. Summer didn't have to primp. That was definitely a sign of a very comfortable relationship.

23.

They were seated in a very comfortable booth in a semi-upscale restaurant. The first course had been whisked away and they waited for their entrée. Summer fidgeted with her silverware. She took a tiny sip of wine and looked up at Jim.

"Jim, what do you think is the meaning of soul?"

Up until that point, they had been talking about mundane subjects. Jim talked about some of his students. Summer talked about her contacts with her publisher. The question caught Jim off guard. He took a deep sip of his wine and thought for a long time.

"Summer, I've never been asked that question before."

"I'm sure you haven't. Most mathematicians are not asked metaphysical questions. Your specialty is the proven. X plus Y equals Z. That's the way it is and there is no question about it. But I'm sure you must think about abstruse things once in a while."

"Well, of course I do. Even in mathematics, everything is not absolutely proven. There are still a lot of questions out there but, eventually, they will be proven by a better brain than mine."

"Okay. Now let's get away from the proven and talk about soul. What do **you** think is the meaning of soul?"

Jim pondered for a minute. He opened his mouth to speak and then shut it and thought again.

"This is a very difficult question, Summer. Right away, when you say soul, I think of phrases that involve the word soul. James Brown is the 'king of soul.' I guess that means that his music comes from his heart. I never thought about it before but I guess that's what it means. The soul of a corporation is the heart of a corporation. It's where all the energy comes from. And, you know what? That's maybe why they call James Brown 'the king of soul.' It's because he puts so much energy into his music. James Brown is not an artist I listen to a lot but I've got to admit that when I hear his music, I've got to do a little toe tapping. I am moved by his songs."

"So does soul mean heart?"

"Okay, Summer, my playful little wordsmith. I guess soul can be called heart but we all know that the heart is an internal organ that pumps blood. It has nothing to do with feelings and where the two coincided, I have no idea. Perhaps that should be the subject of your next book."

Summer laughed. Then she thought about it seriously.

"Let's leave, Jim."

"Summer, we haven't eaten dinner yet."

"Oh, yes, I forgot. Let's leave right after the entrée."

Jim watched Summer pick through her dinner. It was a meal she would totally enjoy in other circumstances but tonight she had other things on her mind. Every once in a while she would look up at him as if to say something but then she would go back to moving the food around on her plate. She would take a nibble every now and then but it was more like eating absent-mindedly rather than savoring every bite.

On the drive home, Jim had some thoughts of his own. He was afraid to approach Summer with the subject. She had been very quiet the whole way home. He was becoming very fond of this woman and was a little nervous that he might not see her again for a long while if he let this chance slip by. Besides, this did sound like an interesting project. He pulled the car up in front of her apartment and turned toward her.

"Summer, I'm pretty sure what's on your mind."

"Oh, I'm sorry, Jim. I must have been acting very rude and ignoring you."

Jim smiled.

"I know a *little* bit about you, Summer Chura. You're ready to start a new book and I'm pretty sure I know what that book is."

"Okay, smartypants, what is it?"

"The minute I said something about the heart and soul coinciding, you clammed up. That's what your book is going to be about. How the organ called a heart came to be identified with soul and emotions."

"Yes, and your statement really provoked me. I had a long talk with my grandmother the other day. She's the one who brought up the subject of soul and got me thinking about it. It has kind of preyed on my mind and when you suggested I write a book about it, the flash went off in my head. Why not research this whole thing? In fact, there is a lot in my Nobel book that can lead me to all kinds of tangents."

"Summer, I'm almost afraid to ask this."

Jim stared ahead through the windshield.

"Afraid to ask what?"

"Can I help you?"

"Can you help me how?"

"Can I help you write your book?"

"Jim, you're a mathematician not a writer."

"Oh, I don't mean I would help you actually write. I would like to help you with your research. As you said, I believe that X plus Y equals Z and there is no changing that. I believe in facts. I can help you by researching and telling you what I believe is a fact, what could be hypothesized, and what I think is garbage even though other people might think it true."

Summer was suddenly overcome with a powerful feeling of déjà vu. She couldn't understand it. She had never had a conversation like this before... or at least not that she could remember. No, it was something else. A circumstance that she couldn't place.

Jim hadn't been sure what Summer's reaction would be but he hadn't expected this long silence. She was somewhere else. Somewhere far, far away in her head. He wasn't sure what to do. Should he break this trance or just wait it out? She shivered and Jim decided to speak.

"Summer, are you cold?"

She turned to face him. Jim had a feeling that she wasn't sure if she knew where she was. She looked at him long and hard and then finally spoke.

"Are you serious about helping me?"

"I wouldn't have brought it up if I wasn't serious."

"Then come on in and let's get busy. I want you to find all the quotes you can find about soul. I'll be making my own notes."

They worked through most of the night. Once in a while, they compared notes but mostly worked independently.

At about four AM, Jim fell asleep on the sofa. Summer had gone into the kitchen for a glass of water and found him there. She quietly covered him with a blanket and tiptoed off to her own room. She had not realized how long they had been working and there was so, so much more to do.

Summer woke up around eleven and discovered that Jim had already made a pot of coffee. He wandered into the kitchen as she was pouring herself a cup.

"Good morning, Sunshine. You ready to go to work again?"

"You bet I am!"

"Okay, but first I'm going to make us some omelets. THEN you can go back to work. After brunch, I would like to run home and shower and change. I'll be back after that and we'll put in a full day."

Jim shook his finger at her.

"But Miss Author, I am not spending the night tonight. I have to go to work tomorrow."

Summer laughed.

"Jim you don't have to stick around today. My gosh, you outdid yourself last night."

"I wanna help and I find this very interesting to see how a famous author like you works. I'm going to be here anytime I can."

Pia waited as long as she could before she called. It was about six p.m. when she could restrain her curiosity any longer. The phone rang about three times before Summer answered.

"Hi, Summer. Just checking up on you to make sure you were okay after your date last night."

"Nice of you to think about me, GrandPi."

"Sooooo, how'd it go?"

"Okay, GrandPi. I think you're getting a little too nosy, but it went very well." Summer couldn't help teasing her grandmother.

"It went so well that he spent the night."

"Hmmmm, you think you should be telling me that?"

"I can tell you that because nothing happened. Jim spent the night because I am working on a new project and he is helping me. We worked so late into the night that he fell asleep on the sofa. I slept in my own bed. So there, GrandPi!"

"Wow, I've got a ton of questions now. The first is – why didn't you invite him into your bed? The second is – what's the new project.?"

"GRANDPI! I am not a fast woman. And the answer to your second question I will not tell you. At least not now."

"It's a book. A new book."

"What makes you think that?"

"First of all, I can hear the excitement in your voice. It's not about your friend – I don't think. It's about an inspiration you have. You get excited about articles you write for the *New Yorker* but you have bigger excitement when you get inspired for a book. I can hear that in your voice now."

"Okay. I will admit it's about another book but I'm not going to tell you what it's about. I will only tell you that you inspired me to write it."

24.

Pia saw Summer infrequently during the next few months. Fortunately, there were family gatherings for birthdays or holidays and Pia was able to be introduced to Jim. She approved of him. She could tell that Jim was 'smitten' by Summer. She was not sure how Summer felt about Jim. She was not a person to wear her heart on her sleeve. Pia tried to pull some information out of Marla. Marla knew no more than she did. Life went on as usual.

Pia could mark it on her calendar. She could remember the exact day. It was the day before Memorial Day. Summer called her up and invited her to lunch. Instead, Pia suggested that Summer join her at her house for lunch. It was going to be a beautiful day and Pia didn't feel like sitting in a restaurant. She hustled around and made a key lime pie, a garden salad, and stirred together the makings of a frittata.

Summer arrived at precisely twelve-thirty. Pia took a long look at her. The girl was so beautiful. She didn't need any makeup which was a good thing since Summer wouldn't take the time to apply much. Her hair was pulled back into a pony tail and she was wearing a tank top, jeans and flip flops. She looked like such a young kid even though she was now almost thirty. Pia noticed that Summer was toting a gift bag.

"Is that for me?"

Summer laughed.

"Now, let's not get greedy. Yes, it is for you but I shall give it to you in due time. What's for lunch? I'm starved."

"I just have to go and finish it up. Sit yourself out on the deck and I'll be right out with frittatas and a salad. What would you like to drink?"

"Oops, I almost forgot. I've got something in my car for us for lunch. Be right back!"

Lickety-split, Summer arrived back in the kitchen with a bottle of Pinot Grigio. It was a very fine bottle of Pinot Grigio.

"Summer, what's behind all this?"

"I am just excited that it's spring and I have the opportunity to be with the best grandmother in the world! Now go cook those frittatas."

Pia thought that Summer was in an extremely good mood. She stirred up the eggs and added some chopped veggies. After putting the mixture in a sauté pan, Pia doled out the salad onto individual plates and toasted the garlic bread.

In the meantime, Summer stretched out her legs as she nestled into the patio chair. She looked around. The lilac blooms were wilting but the peonies were blooming. Signs of daisies were popping up. Pots of plants on the deck were full of blossoms. Purple lavender, gray dusty miller, orange lantana, pink phlox, and red geraniums all presented a kaleidoscope of colors. Most people could not pull off that combination but GrandPi was a wizard when it came to plants. She had a magic touch.

Pia emerged from the sliding glass doors with her arms full. Summer jumped up to help her.

"I think I have everything here, my dear girl, except the wine. Why don't you run in and get it and grab a couple of glasses?"

Settling into their chairs for lunch, Pia kept staring at Summer. She knew that something was up but would let Summer take her sweet old time in telling her. Summer dove into her frittata with relish.

"Oh, GrandPi, this is so good. I was just looking at your plants and thinking what a magic touch you have. But you have it not only with plants but with food, too."

"Thank you."

Pia looked up from her plate with a slight chill running through her body and into Summer's eyes. *The look* was there.

"GrandPi, I've got something for you."

Summer reached down beside her chair and handed the gift bag to Pia.

Pia reached beneath the tissue paper and pulled out a book. She stared at the front cover intently. **Heart and Soul** by Summer Chura.

"My God, Summer, you've got another book published!" She leafed through the pages.

"No, GrandPi. Don't leaf through it. Look at the dedication."

Pia turned the first few pages and read:

"To Pia, who has always been my heart and soul and inspiration. And to Jim, who helped me through many long days and nights and researches. I could not have created this book without either one of them."

There were tears slowly creeping down Pia's face. She could not look at Summer but only stare at the words.

"Why did you refer to me as Pia and not GrandPi or my grandmother?"

"I'm sorry. Are you offended? I didn't mean to offend you. That's the least thing in the world I would do!"

"No, I'm not offended, just curious."

Pia wiped her cheeks with her napkin.

"It just came naturally to me. I wanted to dedicate the book to you and that's what came to mind. Not GrandPi or my grandmother, but just plain Pia."

"Okay, I'll accept that. So Jim helped you a lot, huh?"

"You better believe it!"

Pia took a deep breath.

"GrandPi, you have always taught me a lot. You were the inspiration for the idea of my book. You made me examine my thoughts about a lot of things including what soul means. I did tons of research on this subject. Jim was there with me. He is a mathematician so he doesn't always believe in abstract ideas. We both learned a lot."

"And, without reading your book, what is your conclusion?"

"I'm still not sure but I can sway more with your thinking."

"Why is that?"

"I'll show you why."

Summer fumbled in her pocket for something and then held her hands in her lap for a minute. Finally she brought her left hand up to the table and held it towards her grandmother. On the ring finger was a beautiful diamond.

"Oh, Summer, I am so happy for you!"

Pia reached across and held Summer's hand and more tears dribbled from her eyes.

"Please don't cry, GrandPi. I still am not convinced if it's chemicals or soul or what but it works. Can you believe? I love Jim and he loves me."

"I'm very happy for you." Pia said solemnly.

"GRANDPI! I thought you would be more excited than this."

"I am very excited for you, my love. I don't know what's come over me. Maybe, I'm afraid I've lost you to Jim."

"Good heavens! You will never lose me to anyone. I have to tell you about this, GrandPi. It's because you are always so right."

"I'm not always right. I just pretend that I am."

"Well, you were right about this. Let me put it in order. When I first met Jim, I was attracted to him. Perhaps that was the chemicals. We worked really well together. Perhaps that's more chemicals. And then I found things happening to me. I was blossoming. Just like your flowers! When flowers start, they start chemically. They are pollinated. And then they bloom into gorgeous creations."

Summer swept her arm toward Pia's yard to demonstrate.

"Is that soul, GrandPi?"

"Summer, you've always been a gorgeous flower."

"No, no, no. Maybe to you I was but not to me. I now feel personally that I am a gorgeous flower."

Pia smiled but didn't say anything.

"GrandPi, you just don't know. I feel more alive, more creative, and beautiful. No, I bet you do understand. You had that with my grandfather, didn't you? That's why you are such a beautiful flower now."

"I'm afraid I'm on the waning edge of the flower now. My petals are starting to droop."

"No, you've still got tons of petals left. But you didn't answer my question, GrandPi. Is what I feel- soul?"

"You wrote the book about it. What do you think?"

"It's amazing. My Nobelist book was about folklore, myths and religion – how people depended on those stories and carved their lives around those stories. Could soul be included in that?"

"Summer, it's what you want to think. It seems to me that you have always believed in yourself. You have achieved quite a bit for someone who has not believed that she has bloomed."

"But that's on the competitive edge. I always wanted to super excel in school. If you remember correctly, I divulged to you – after winning the Nobel prize – what would I do now to top that."

"And I believe I said to you something like you could win another one."

Pia paused for a long time and then looked straight into her granddaughter's eyes.

"I also believe that I said something about finding a man in your life."

For a brief second, Summer gave her *the look* and then shrugged her shoulders. "Okay, what's for dessert?"

"What do you think a fading flower would make for a beautiful rosebud?"

"Key lime pie!" Summer clapped her hands together like a child.

After Summer left, Pia laid down on her bed and cried. She really cried. Sobbing crying. She didn't know why. It was totally a mixture of emotions. She was so happy for Summer. Was Summer a reincarnation of Hugh? Was Hugh communicating to her through Summer? It was all so confusing. It was a persistence of memory. The thought made her think of the famous painting by Dali. The melting clocks. And that reminded her of the faces of Summer and Hugh fading in and out during the Nobel award ceremony.

Then there was this other thing. She had been to the doctor on a routine check-up. Pia had felt very healthy except for the aches and pains of someone getting older. She had advanced cancer. She didn't know how long she had, and she had told no one.

25.

She knew she was dying. Everyone was around her hospital bed. Marla was holding her right hand. Eric was holding her left hand. And there was Summer. Summer looked so happy even though she was sad. She finally had a man to love. They were holding hands. Pia was so happy for Summer. And she could see all her other grandchildren. They were all there. *What the hell for? They should all be out playing tennis or riding in their boats or hiking in the Rockies. Why are they all here? Oh, yes. I am dying.* They had all come to pay their respects and be with her.

Although her eyes were closed, she could still see Summer standing there , radiant because she was finally in love. It pleased Pia. She tried vainly to open her eyes and look at Summer but she couldn't. Soon she would know. She would know when she got to wherever she was going. Was there reincarnation? Was there a communication between the dead and the living? There was one last refrain left in her head.

"And when I die and when I'm dead, dead and gone, there'll be one child born in a world to carry on, carry on."

Summer was frantically packing up bags to take to the pool. Her little two year old toddler, Hugh, was constantly getting in her way – as toddlers do. She checked her wallet for the pool pass. And that's when she saw it. She didn't know why she had not come across it in the past few years. But there it was.

The strangest thing was that it was not in GrandPi's handwriting but in grandfather Hugh's penmanship. She sat on the floor and cried.

Little Hugh came and put his arms around her neck. "What's wrong, Mommy?"

"Nothing is wrong, honey. Everything is right." She looked at the piece of paper again.

"And if I go when you're still here....
Know that I still live on,
Vibrating to a different measure
Behind a thin veil that you cannot see through.
Yes, you cannot see me
So you must have faith.
I wait the time when we can soar together again,
Both aware of each other,
Until then, live your life to the fullest,
And when you need me
Just whisper my name in your heart
............I will be there."